YURI'S BRUSH
WITH MAGIC

Maureen Crane Wartski

For Michael and
Aidan —
may your world be full
of magic —
M. [signature] 7/14/11

SLEEPY HOLLOW BOOKS
Durham, North Carolina

Sleepy Hollow Books
Durham, North Carolina 27705
www.sleepyhollowbooks.com

Library of Congress Control Number: 2010936438
ISBN 978-0-9824542-51 (pbk.)

FIRST EDITION, November 2010
Printed in the United States of America
10 9 8 7 6 5 4 3 2 1

Book design and typesetting by Dave Wofford of Horse & Buggy Press
Cover illustrations by Jason Strutz
Sumi brush painting of frontispiece turtle by Jinxiu Zhao
Special thanks for beginning cover concept to Yael Jacobson,
and to Claudia Gabel and Melinda Ruley for editorial consultation.

Remembering Aunt Juliette F. Schweri —

artist, storyteller

Children's Song

Too—rian-se
To-o-rian-se, To-o-rian-se
Koko wa doko no hoso-michi ja?
Tenjin-sama no hoso-michi ja!
Chiito-to-o—shite kuda-shan-se?
Goyo-o no nai mono to-o-sha-senu
Kono ko no nana-tsu no oiwai ni
O fuda wo o-same ni mai-ri-masu!
Iki wa yoi yoi, kae-ri-wa kowai...
Kowai naga-ra mo to-o-riyanse to-o-rianse!

Pass, pass
Where does this narrow path lead?
It's the path to the Tenjin shrine.
Please let us through.
We don't let people who have no business through.
This child is now seven years old,
And we have come to make an offering.
Going is safe ... returning is scary!
If you are prepared for this, pass ... pass!

Chapter 1

LAST NIGHT I DREAMED that I was singing Mama's song. I woke up with all the music in my head, but before my eyes were open, it had all gone except for a memory that was about as real as a puff of smoke.

I was trying to remember when Ken stuck his head around my door and told me that I'd been making noises like a frog.

My brother acted as if he was Somebody just because he was twelve—not even three years older than me. He wasn't big enough to push me around, so on my way out the door, I hip-checked him hard, caught him off guard and really made him stagger. Then I went into the kitchen and found Dad hanging up the phone.

"Your mother spent a peaceful night, Tammy," he reported. "No change."

Our mother had been in a coma for more than two months, ever since a man in a big hurry jumped a red light and smashed into her car. At first the doctors had been hopeful that Mama *would* wake up, but now they didn't sound so positive.

Mrs. Lauria, our sitter, tried to cheer us up. She said we should never mind the doctors because they didn't know everything. But Dad took us to visit Mama every weekend and there never was any change.

Nothing had changed this morning either. Dad looked so tired and discouraged that I poured him some juice and took it to him.

He said, "Thank you, Littlebit." Then he sat down at the kitchen table and cleared his throat.

"Tammy, what would you say if I told you that today was your last day at camp?"

"You mean she's going to stay home?" Ken came sailing into the kitchen, nearly knocking down the carton of OJ and making a neat, one-handed save. "No way. I'm not looking after her."

"Calm down," Dad said, but Ken kept moving around the kitchen, tossing the OJ carton from one hand to another. "I said, *calm down!*" Dad roared. Dad hardly ever raised his voice. Ken dropped into a chair just as shocked as I was. Dad stared hard at Ken, who tried to meet his eyes, but couldn't.

"How would you and Tammy like to go to the beach for the rest of the summer?"

"Really?"

"You're messing with us, Dad, right?"

Both of us spoke at once, Ken's voice starting deep and cracking high in the way he hated. Dad almost smiled at our surprise, but the smile never got up to his eyes.

"I tell you what, while the rest of us are burning up, you'll be paddling and surfing and watching the sun set down into the ocean."

Well, that didn't sound so bad. We'd spent a weekend at Topsail Island a couple of years back, and it was fun...

"But if you're taking us to the beach, what about Mama?" I objected. "Raleigh is so far from the beach. How'll you visit her?"

"I'd give my eyeteeth to go with you." Suddenly, it seemed that Dad was having trouble meeting our eyes. "Look, you'll be staying in a house right on the beach. Not second row, not third, but beachfront. Your aunt Yuri has rented that house for the summer, and..."

"Who?"

"Your aunt Yuri," Dad said, too heartily. "Technically, though, Yuri Hamada is your grand aunt, your Nana Honey's younger sister," he added.

I was slow to understand, but Ken was quicker. "Wait a minute. Are you talking about Mean Yuri?"

Every family has its own special story, Mama used to say. I guess Mean Yuri Hamada was ours. Ken and I had heard a million times about our Nana Honey's nasty younger sister. We'd grown up watching our grandmother cry whenever she talked about this Yuri.

And now Dad wanted us to stay with this mean old woman? "Don't call her that," Dad was saying. "It's disrespectful."

"But—but aren't you talking about Mean Yuri?" Ken demanded. "The one who hated our Nana just because she married an American? The sister who swore never to talk to Nana again and never answered her letters?"

Dad cleared his throat. "Miss Yuri Hamada and your grandmother may have had their differences, but that's in the past. She explained about the letters. She never got them, you see..."

"You called her a mean hag, too," I interrupted. "I heard you telling Mama."

Dad sighed and said let that be a lesson to us to keep our words sweet, "Otherwise, someday you might have to eat them."

Ken said he'd rather be in jail than stay two days with Mean Yuri. "Anyway," I added hopefully, "we can't talk to her. We can't speak Japanese."

"She speaks perfect English," Dad insisted. "Miss Yuri telephoned me a week ago. She's coming to the States to work on some paintings. Since she knew we live in North Carolina, she decided to paint at Emerald Isle. She's an artist, you know. A famous one."

What did we care what she was? And what did *she* care about us?

"She asked what she could do to help," Dad was saying. "She's sincere. She told me that she's renting a house at the beach this July and August, and she'd like you two to stay with her.

"Look," Dad broke off to add, "your mother always says that things happen for a reason. This is proof of that. I was going out of my mind not knowing what I was going to do with you during the summer, and then Miss Yuri phoned. It's Providence. And quit calling her names, hear me? You're staying with her, so get used to it."

The room got very quiet. Dad just sat there so still that the kitchen brimmed with a silence so heavy and thick it became hard to breathe.

"But we want to stay here with you," I whispered.

He wrapped his arms around me and held me tight. I could feel the thump-bump of his heart. "Tammy, he said, "we all have to do things we don't want to do. No matter what went on between Miss Yuri and your Nana, Yuri's your aunty. She'll take care of you. In case..."

He broke off. Glancing at Ken, I saw that the stubborn lines of his face had melted into fear. "Mama's worse?" he croaked.

Son, we have to face it—the longer she stays in her coma, the less chance there is that she'll wake up." Dad looked down at me. "Littlebit, you have to be my brave girl tomorrow, understand? I want to take you both to see Mama before you leave for the beach. Miss Yuri's going to meet us at Tall Oaks."

Chapter 2

THOUGHTS OF MEAN YURI HAMADA stayed with me all day.

Without me inviting her, our Nana's rotten sister snuck into everything I did, especially my packing. I tried to make things better by putting a framed photo of Mama in my suitcase. After that, I carefully lifted the music box Nana Honey had given me from its special place on my dresser. Grandpa Louis ordered the small, silver box from Japan for Nana, and it plays our 'Going Is Easy' song. It's very old and precious, so I usually don't move it much, but this was an emergency.

Mean Yuri Hamada! Even when I said my bedtime prayers there she was, a short, ugly, evil-eyed Nastiness. Mean Yuri actually got mixed into my dreams, which were about the sea, and waves that were so huge and so tall that they covered the whole earth and blotted out any echo of Mama's song.

I wish now that I'd written Mama's song in my good notebook where I copy my best stories. It wasn't a song that many people would know, being that it was an old Japanese folk song that our grandmother, Nana Honey, had taught our mother.

Someday I am going to write about Nana Honey, too. She died when I was just five, but I remember how beautiful she was. She had long hair that was still black even when she got old, and a voice that sang even when she was just talking. Mama has brown hair and green eyes like Grandpa, and Ken is like her. But I have Nana's eyes. Whenever I looked in the mirror, I could see my eyes were so brown they were almost black.

Maybe I should explain that Nana Honey was Japanese. She had been born in Japan, so of course the song she sang was in Japanese, too. Mama translated it for me, and one of the lines I remember went, "The going is easy, coming back is scary." Mama said that the song was part of a game, like our Red Rover.

'Red Rover, come over...' and Mean Yuri was coming! Even the thought that I was going to see Mama was spoiled by knowing that we had to leave for the beach right after our visit.

The next day at Tall Oaks my nerves skittered and my stomach began to turn cartwheels. "Take deep breaths," Ken whispered as we walked through corridor after corridor to the elevator. "Don't you lose it, Tam."

"Now, remember what I told you, Tammy," Dad added as the elevator doors slid open at the third floor. "You have to be a brave girl."

I grit my teeth hard, balled up my fists, and walked stiff-legged into the room, and there she was dressed in a pretty pink nightgown with her brown hair spread out over the pillow. I didn't look at the IV in her hand, I looked at her sweet face instead. Her cheeks were pink, her mouth relaxed, and her eyelids fluttered a little as if she wasn't in a coma ... as if she was getting ready to wake up.

"Mama," I whispered, and touched her hand. It was warm, and I closed my eyes and remembered the last time she'd hugged me, her cheek warm against mine, and her voice saying my name.

Ken started telling her about his week, sounding almost normal. I wanted to talk to her, too, but the words wouldn't come, so I just stroked her hand and listened to Ken talking and then to Dad, who said that Ken and I were going away to the beach for a while.

"We love you, Lily," Dad said, and he kissed her. "We're waiting for you to come back to us, sugar."

When we left the room, Ken was wiping his eyes with the back of his hand, but my tears were all balled together in my throat so I could hardly breathe. Nobody spoke on the elevator going down. When we got out, Dad sort of looked around in an unsure way until a husky voice said, "James Jennings?"

A tall, thin Asian lady was standing not far from us. She was wearing a dark blue blouse and a long, dark, flowing skirt. Her gray hair was tied up in a knot at the back of her head. Dark eyes, set under flaring eyebrows, were intent and watchful.

"Miss Yuri?" Dad said. He sounded both nervous and relieved.

"Yes, that is me." She came walking toward us, holding out her hand. Dad shook it, and they looked each other over. "I am pleased to make your acquaintance," the thin lady said, formally. "These are the children?"

Dad put his arms around Ken and me, naming us. Then he added, "This is your aunt Yuri."

"Kenjiro and Tamako. We will spend the summer together, *ne* ... isn't that so?" Mean Yuri Hamada spoke clearly and quickly, but you could tell English wasn't her language by the way she mispronounced some words and twisted others around her tongue as if trying them out and not liking how they tasted. She'd also called us by names Nana Honey had sometimes used. "We don't know each other," she went on, "but we are family."

From the way Ken's mouth had tightened, I knew what he was thinking. *So where were you all those years when our Nana needed you?* "Our names are Ken and Tammy," he said, shortly.

Dad prodded us, so we mumbled greetings. Yuri Hamada gave us a deep-set, unblinking stare for another minute, and then she turned back to Dad. "I have gone up already to see Lily," she said in her deep voice. "I thought, best to go alone." Dad nodded. "Is there hope she may recover?"

Most people dropped their voices when asking that question, but our so-called aunt spoke casually as if asking the price of something in a store.

"We have to believe that there's always hope," Dad said.

Mean Yuri then looked at her wristwatch. "It's a long drive to the ocean, so we should start at once."

"Da-ad…"

He hugged me tight. "I need you to be my big girl, Tammy. Ken, you listen to your aunt and do whatever she says. I'll call you every evening, I promise."

Chapter 3

WE NEARLY NEVER MADE IT to the beach. Although she didn't exactly look mental, Mean Yuri was a crazy driver. She pushed that little gray car along as if she was some kind of NASCAR speed demon. Zip! She was in one lane. Zap! She was in another. When she blared her horn ordering a huge eighteen-wheeler out of her way, I closed my eyes, and Ken, who'd been set on ignoring her the whole trip blurted for her to watch it.

Mean Yuri muttered something we couldn't understand. "Don't worry," she called over her shoulder, "I've been driving for many years in Osaka traffic."

"How many cars did you smash up?" Ken gasped.

"What's that? I can't hear you." Then she said, "Why do you Americans have to drive on the wrong side of the road?"

I closed my eyes and felt my stomach roll from side to side. When I moaned, Ken said in a fake-polite voice, "Could you slow down, please, ma'am? My sister's going to barf all over the back seat."

"Car sick, ha?" Yuri took one hand off the steering wheel and rummaged in her purse. "Here!"

A package came sailing into my lap. Inside were small, dry, yellowish chunks of disgusting-looking *something*. I looked at Ken, who made a gagging sound and shook his head. "It's candy. Won't hurt you, so take."

It was a command. I took a tiny piece of whatever it was and popped it into my mouth. First came a sugary taste and then fire. "Candied ginger," our mental aunt explained, as I coughed. "It will settle you down right away."

Settle me down? My stomach was churning worse than before, and I bet I was turning green from the way Ken had moved to the farthest edge of the car. "Ginger," Yuri was saying, "is wonderful. Cures car sickness. Cures bad stomach. One time, ginger bought a gold mine. Did you hear the story about that?"

Ken said "No," in a cold, discouraging voice, which apparently didn't get through to Mean Yuri, who began,

"Many years ago in Japan there was a poor man who sold ginger to make his living. He had to work extra hard because he had sickly old parents to support and three unmarried sisters who needed to find good husbands. Not an easy thing, not then and not now."

"So why didn't he give up?" Ken growled.

"What? Give up and let his family starve and his sisters turn into Old Misses? Never! That poor ginger man worked from morning 'til night walking all over Japan to sell his goods. Most of the time he worked alone, but one day he chanced to meet a friend, a man who sold fishing nets. Together they tramped up and down a tall mountain trying to make sales. Peddling isn't easy work, and after a whole day's effort they were tired out and discouraged. *'Mo yada!'* groaned the seller of nets. 'I've had it. I am going to take a nap.'"

Ken yawned loudly, closed his eyes and pretended to fall asleep.

"So, right away, the net seller began to snore, but our friend the ginger peddler was too worried to sleep." Yuri yanked the steering wheel to the left and pulled in front of a pickup truck. The driver blared his horn, and she shook her head and said that some people had no manners. "Instead of resting, he remained wide-eyed awake and that is why he came to see a big bumble bee fly into his friend's nose—and out again."

"Gross!" Ken sputtered. "That is so totally—look, *ma'am,* I don't want to hear this story if that's okay with you."

"In and out, in and out," Yuri chanted in her husky voice. "That bumble bee was a busy fellow. Finally, the sleeper awakened and said he'd had a dream. In the dream, a bee had told him where a lot of gold was buried in the mountains. Most people would have laughed, just as you are doing now, Ken, but the ginger peddler man chose to believe. He offered his friend the only thing he had—all his ginger—in order to buy the directions to that buried gold."

"And I guess he found it and got rich?"

"Not right away. The ginger peddler worked and dug and worked and dug for weeks and weeks. People laughed at him, called him a crazy person, and made fun of him. Still he worked. Many times he was so tired and hungry he was ready to drop down dead, but he kept at it. He had determination and heart not to mention old parents and three unmarried sisters! And, most important, he had hope. You see? No matter how difficult life came to be, he believed that all would be well!"

Yuri told us that in the end the ginger seller man found so much gold that his parents were never poor again. "His sisters all married princes and lords," she added, "and the wedding feasts were wonderful. Fifteen appetizers and twenty main courses and desserts like dumplings and sweet bean cakes and ice cream sodas— ("That's totally so stupid," Ken spluttered to me. "She doesn't know what she's talking about. I bet they didn't have ice cream sodas back then.")—which means you have to believe in dreams. *Ne?* Hold onto them even when it becomes impossible to hope."

Mean Yuri continued to talk, but her voice seemed to be sliding away. The knots in my stomach were easing out, and my eyelids had begun to feel heavy— like the eyes of the man who sold nets. *Even when it's impossible to hope,* she'd said. I thought about that as I slid away into sleep.

Chapter 4

ROAR, SLAP, POUND!

I blinked awake to the sound of the sea. The car had stopped and the passenger door was wide open.

Ken was already out of the car. I could see him standing on top of a stone wall. When I unbuckled myself, the first thing I saw was a big, brown, ugly old house perched on tall poles. A bunch of steps led up to a bright blue door.

Yuri came out of that door and walked down the steps toward me. "I guess ginger did its work," she said. "So. What do you think of the house?"

"It's fine," I mumbled.

She sent me a sideways look. "It is ugliest thing I ever saw. But the real estate people said it was high season, and if I wanted a house right on the beach, this was the best they can do for me."

Now she looked me up and down. "You remind me of my sister," she said. I allowed that a lot of people said I looked like Nana Honey. "That's right—'*Mitsu*' translates to 'honey' in your language," Yuri said. She was quiet for a second and then asked, "Did you know that your mother was named for me? A lily is *yuri* in Japanese."

She was smiling. A surprise. 'Til now she'd looked stern, but when she smiled, her face changed. Though she didn't look at all like Nana Honey, there was something there that made me think of her. Something faint that slipped away as she said, "Let's get inside."

She opened the trunk. There were our suitcases crammed in along with an easel and a big old sketchbook plus a whole mess of other stuff. Next she shouted for Ken, who reluctantly hopped down from the wall and helped to carry our stuff into the house. There was a lot of stuff. While Yuri shouted orders, we carried everything through the kitchen, past a big, many-windowed room with overstuffed chairs and an old TV, and down a hall to the first of four doors.

"My studio," Yuri announced. "Put all of those things down over there by the desk. Carefully, I said."

Finally it was over. Our suitcases were in the house, and Mean Yuri's easel was up in her studio, her sketchbook was on a table by the window, and she was done fussing with her paints and brushes.

She assigned us our rooms. The one nearest her 'studio' was hers. Ken's bedroom was on the left side of the hall, mine was on the right. Yuri Hamada's bedroom connected to a bathroom while Ken and I shared the one in the hall.

"Is that satisfactory?" she asked. Ken shrugged; I nodded. "Good. Unpack yourselves, and meanwhile I will make some lunch."

My room was smaller than my bedroom back at home. There was a bed, a bureau with rattly drawers, and a small desk near a window. Through the window I could see some tall pine trees. Suddenly homesick enough to die, I leaned my head against the rough wood of the windowsill. I couldn't do this. I wanted to go home.

"Lunch!" Yuri shouted.

Eating was the last thing I wanted to do. I brushed away the wet from my eyes as Ken came into the room and walked over to stand beside me. "Lousy view," he commented. I nodded, hoping he wouldn't notice that I'd been crying. "Look, Tam," he then said, "I have an idea of how we can get out of here."

Ken said that if we acted really ugly, Yuri would get mad enough to send us home.

Something told me that Yuri wasn't one to cave easily. I told him so and he said, "We'll just see about that."

"We'd be in so much trouble..."

"But we'd be home. We'd be near Mama, and away from her. We've got to do this together, okay, Tam?" Ken insisted. "We have to work her at the same time."

He broke off as Yuri stuck her head in the door and demanded, had we heard her calling us? "In Japan, when somebody makes a meal for you, you are thankful."

"Well, we're not in Japan," Ken shot back.

I thought she was going to lay him out for sassing her, but instead she turned and walked back down the hall. Ken looked pleased with himself, but my stomach did a couple of flipovers as we followed our mean aunt into the kitchen. There were plates on the small, round kitchen table, and bread, and cheese, and apples, and peanut butter.

"You must be hungry," was all she said.

Wary of her, we made ourselves sandwiches and ate while she poured milk for us, and a glass of bottled water for herself. Then she peeled an apple, sliced it, and spread it with peanut butter. "It's good," she said.

"I thought..." I began, then stopped, feeling dumb.

"Did you think that I only ate rice and raw fish?" Yuri clicked her tongue. "We don't know each other."

"Not our fault, is it?"

Again, she ignored Ken. "I am not used to children. I am an Old Miss. All my life, I studied art and not communication skills. So we must become used to each other, otherwise the summer will be long, hot and very bad."

Leaning back, she clasped her hands together and set them in the lap of her flowing dark skirt. "So. Let me tell you about myself. My name is Yuri Hamada, and I'm an artist. I am sixty-eight years old. My home is in Nishi-nomiya, which is a city in Japan. I have studied art in London, in Paris, and in Firenze, which is in Italia."

Ken and I exchanged glances. Was she trying to impress us?

"Your turn to tell about yourself," she was saying.

"This is stupid," Ken protested.

"Is it more smart to say nothing and glare?" Yuri came right back. "You said that it wasn't your fault that we don't know each other. This is your chance. Tell me about yourself, Ken."

I could see Ken turning things over in his head. Should he play her game or not? Finally, he shrugged and said, "I'm Kenneth L. Jennings, *not* Kenjiro. I'm a student at Ashland Middle School. I'm old enough not to get asked a lot of stupid questions."

Ken's ears had turned pink—he really wasn't used to sassing people—but Yuri paid that no mind and asked him about his hobbies and whether he enjoyed sports and what he wanted to be when he grew up. "I want to be an avatar in a video game," was Ken's answer.

For a second, she looked as if she was going to call him on that, but she didn't. Now it was my turn. "Tamara Louise Jennings. I go to Ashland West." I'd been all set to follow Ken's lead and say I wanted to be a lady wrestler, but under Yuri's cool gaze I felt myself starting to wilt. Reluctantly, I mumbled that I liked to write stories and stuff.

Yuri nodded. "Ah, a writer. That is the basis, then. So. To learn, we have to ask questions as well as give information. Ken Jennings, what would you like to know about me?"

My brother cleared his throat. "How come you speak English? You told Nana Honey you hated America and Americans, didn't you? You told her you never wanted to see her again."

"I said those things during the heat of argument. I was very young, much younger than you are," Yuri replied, real cool. "I learned to speak English in London. It is the language of business. My turn to ask. Tammy, what sort of stories do you like to write?"

For the next five minutes she grilled me. When I'd mumbled my way through the worst of the questions, Ken was ready for her. "How come you never wrote to Nana Honey?" Mean Yuri said nothing. "She talked about you all the time, said you were her smart little sister." Ken's voice kept getting louder and louder until he was almost yelling. "You just ignored her," he accused. "Like she'd died or something."

"I have explained to your papa that my father kept all of Mitsu's—Nana Honey's—letters from me, so I never knew where she had gone." Yuri frowned. "You must realize what happened. In my parents' eyes, Mitsu *was* dead. When she married Louis Laverre, our father had Mitsu's name removed from the family registry."

"He did what?" I asked, but nobody heard me. Ken and Yuri had locked eyes and neither of them was letting go.

"And you agreed with that?" Ken said. His voice cracked, but he didn't even notice. "You wanted her dead?"

"Only one question allowed," Mean Yuri snapped. "My turn. What did Mitsu say about me?"

"She was sad you never wrote," I put in before Ken could speak. "She wrote you lots of letters, and they all came back unopened." I saw Yuri Hamada blink sharply. "Nana Honey cried because she missed you so much..."

Yuri abruptly got to her feet, swept up her apple and water glass. "I am going to paint, now," she flung over her shoulder. "You can walk onto the beach if you wish, but do not go in the water. Understand me? Not when I am not there." She wheeled around to face us, her eyes as hard as black stones. "Are you little babies who must be watched all the time, or can I trust you to do as I say?"

We nodded. Me, grateful that the questioning was over, Ken pleased that he'd gotten her so riled. "Whatever," he drawled. "Come on, Tam, let's go outside."

The house we were staying in had a front porch that we could get to through sliding glass doors on one side of the kitchen. The porch had been newly painted blue, like the front door. Out there we could see the ocean close enough to watch the wave troughs foam into white caps.

We ran down the porch steps to a boardwalk. It took us over the tall sand dune, across a gully overgrown with grass and sea oats, and finally onto the beach.

"Sweet!" Ken exclaimed. "When the tide comes in, the waves'll come up right to the boardwalk."

He pulled off his sneakers and raced across the sand toward the water. I followed, stopping to check out the big, brown and white shells scattered along the tide line. As I bent to pick one up, waves curled around my bare feet then tugged away so sharply that I staggered.

"Watch that undertow," Ken warned, "It's pretty mean."

We stood shoulder to shoulder while the waves came in and dragged out. Whatever we thought of Mean Yuri Hamada, the beach was excellent. The late afternoon sky was Carolina blue, and gulls were dipping down mewing and screeching. Then came a line of bigger birds— pelicans—that skimmed the water so close that they were belly-to-belly with the waves. "They're a family," Ken said.

Suddenly I missed Mama and Dad so much that I ached all over. I closed my eyes and tried to imagine them with us—Dad reading a book on a beach chair while Mama collected shells along the shore.

Ken shoved me, breaking the spell. "Last one's a lizard's tail!" he yelled over his shoulder.

I followed shouting that it wasn't fair—he'd gotten a head start—and after a while slowed down to enjoy the beach. It really was a cool place. Little kids ran in and out of tide-pools or built sandcastles, people were sunbathing or standing in the surf and fishing, and many of the fishermen smiled at me and said 'hey,' in a friendly way.

I was just about to plop down on the warm sand when I saw a small area blocked off with stakes and rope. I went closer and I saw that there was also a small sign numbered "8." Underneath the number was something that said it was against federal law to mess with loggerhead turtles or their nests.

Where were the turtles? I leaned over the roped-off area and peered around. There was nothing to see except sand. Were there turtles here buried under the sand? Squatting down, I touched the sand with my fingertip.

"Stop that this instant!"

Spinning around too quickly, I landed on my butt. From that embarrassing position I blinked up at a redheaded lady, who was standing there glaring at me with her hands on the hips of her snug, lime-green Capri pants.

Chapter 5

"DIDN'T YOU SEE THE SIGN?" the lady shrieked. Red-painted toes in leather sandals did an impatient tap-tap. "Can't you *read* that disturbing an endangered species is against the *law*?"

Snickers—and then a "braa-haa-ha!" laugh came from a kid standing a few feet away. He was about Ken's age but built like the Pillsbury™ dough boy, short and spongy. He had red hair that was cut so that it sat on the top of his head like a saucer. Still laughing, he popped out a balloon of purple bubble gum.

"Did you hear what I *said?*" the redheaded lady demanded.

"Maybe she's deaf and dumber, Grandma," the kid sneered.

"Now, Halsey, you hush," the lady said, but without any punch to the words. "What I asked *you*, miss, is whether you read what that sign says." She waited for my nod and then added, "If you mess with that nest again, you will be arrested!"

She stalked off. Halsey moved up close to me and blew bubblegum-breath at me. "You heard her, right, dummy?"

I pushed him away from me, and he said a bad word and shoved me, hard. Flat out on the sand again, I heard a drumbeat of footsteps. Then Halsey went flying backward, and Ken was standing over him.

"You touch my sister again, and I'll make fish-bait out of you," Ken gritted.

There was a squawk. Here came the redheaded lady galumphing through the sand and yelling for Ken to leave her grandbaby alone. "You monster," she shouted, "I'll call the police. I'll have you arrested!"

She fell on her knees beside Halsey, who was digging sand out of his ears, and begged him to tell her, was he injured? Ken grabbed my wrists and hauled me up like a sack of potatoes. "C'mon, Tam, let's go."

"You'll go to the police station!" Halsey's grandma began, but then another voice interrupted and said for everyone to calm down.

A man was making his way down the steps of a nearby boardwalk. He had white hair that jutted out from under a Boston Red Sox baseball cap, wore jeans cut off at the knees, and had a beach towel slung over his shoulders. He was leaning on a metal cane.

"Now, let's just calm down," he repeated. "You want to watch your blood pressure in this heat, Mrs. Fowler."

He negotiated the last few steps, balanced himself on his stick, and then started shambling toward us. Meantime, the redheaded lady was sputtering about Ken being dangerous and evil. "If you'd seen what he was doing to my Halsey, Mr. Knitsbridge..."

"Looked to me that the boy was defending his little sister," the man said, interrupting so smoothly that I was impressed. "Halsey pushed the young lady..."

"What young lady?" old Halsey sneered.

"...And her big brother came to her defense." Close up, I could see that Mr. Knitsbridge's hair was sun-bleached blond. Though he was pretty old, his eyes were bright blue and held a twinkle as if he knew more than he let on. He was tall and healthy looking except for his left leg, which was scarred something terrible and splayed out so that the toes pointed away from the body. He wasn't from around here, I could tell.

Instead of letting words flow in a natural way, he chopped them hard enough to hurt. But he had a good voice clear and calm as though he was used to being listened to.

"Now," Mr. Knitsbridge was saying, "where I come from, a man's got the right to defend his family."

Well, that redheaded Mrs. Fowler sputtered for a minute. Then she snapped to and told Halsey they were going home. "I'd better not catch you near my grandson again," she warned Ken. "And you," she added to me, "stay away from the turtle eggs!"

"Who does she think she is?" Ken growled, but Mr. Knitsbridge put a hand on his shoulder that said, be quiet.

"Tell you what Mrs. Fowler was all worked up about," he explained. "That sign warns everyone that a female loggerhead came up on this beach and laid her eggs. The #8 means hers was the eighth nest recorded. I know because I saw her nesting and recorded the date. April 30th."

I'd never thought much about turtles before, but the way Mr. Knitsbridge's face lit up when he talked made them sound interesting. "You *saw* her lay her eggs?" I asked.

"Yes ma'am, and took her photo, too. You see standing before you a volunteer for the Emerald Isle Turtle Protection Program." He straightened up a bit and tugged at the brim of his cap.

Mr. Knitsbridge explained that a turtle's eggs took about 55 days, give or take, to hatch. Starting in May it was his job to walk this section of beach. If he saw any sign of nesting activity, he reported this to one of the permit holders, the only people who were allowed to handle the nests or the turtles.

"Then in July or August," he added, "things really get exciting. The eggs hatch and the little turtles try and get to the sea. Sometimes they do, sometimes crabs or other predators get them. That's why we try to be on hand— to get them safely on their way."

I asked if Mrs. Fowler was a volunteer, too, and he said no, just a concerned citizen who just happened to live next door to him. Which, judging from his expression, was something he didn't like much.

Who would? But our new friend was still talking about turtles. He said that if the hatchlings survived, they'd come back to their birth-beaches to lay their eggs.

"Do they really remember where they were hatched, Mr. Knitsbridge?"

"Call me Sol," he said, "The way I understand it, instinct drives female turtles to return to a beach in the same region where they were born. So a turtle produced from a nest in Emerald may come back as an adult and lay her nest in Cape Hatteras or Bald Head Island, or even South Carolina. Some of the hatchlings from #8 will be back. The strong ones, anyway. Natural selection."

We talked turtles for a while longer. Then Ken thanked him for standing up for us. "Anytime," Mr. Sol said as Ken, suddenly all stiff and formal, shook his hand. Then he added, "Well—time for my afternoon swim."

"What's natural selection?" I asked as Mr. Sol headed off for the water. Ken started to explain how weak and slow turtles got weeded out by becoming a part of the food chain. I dug my toes into the sand, frowning. The thought of baby turtles being eaten made me feel queasy.

"That's just the way it is, Tam," Ken said. "If a turtle's too weak, it won't make it out there."

Out there was the huge ocean. I was staring out at the horizon when I heard something behind me. I glanced over my shoulder and there was Halsey on the boardwalk, shambling and shaking out a cruel imitation of Mr. Sol's walk.

"What a creep!" I cried.

"Yeah. He better not come anywhere near us," Ken added, scowling. "Bad enough we have Mean Yuri on our back. We don't need that twerp, too."

Chapter 6

DAD CALLED US AT SEVEN, just as he'd promised. He didn't have much news except that Mama'd had a good day. After that we had dinner. Ken kept the pressure on Yuri, complaining that he hated tomato soup and that the store-bought rolls were disgusting. Doing my bit, I whined about how good a cook Nana Honey had been. Yuri replied that we should be grateful for our food and that if we were hungry enough, we'd eat anything.

"So, how would you know that?" Ken snorted. "Have you been hungry?"

Yuri looked at him, stone-faced, and said, "Yes, I have." Then she said she was going to get some work done, stalked off to her studio, and slammed the door.

Ken did a Super Bowl shimmy, he was so pleased with himself. According to him, Mean Yuri would cave in and send us home in a few days. "But we've got to keep the pressure on," he warned me. "We have to do whatever it takes."

Ken cranked up the radio and started singing and hopping around the room. If she heard him carrying on, though, she didn't let on. She stayed in her studio with the door closed all evening. She didn't even tell us what time to go to bed. Ken was for staying up all night, but my eyes were closing, so I headed for my room. "Whatever it takes to get us home," Ken reminded me.

To concentrate on hating Mean Yuri, I took out the music box that Nana had given me and played the 'going is easy' tune over and over. The box was so old that there was a little catch every so often, and it made me think of how Nana Honey had carried me onto her front porch one July night, and sat us down in the white rocker that Grandpa had made for her. Then she'd pointed out two bright stars in the sky and told me the story of how these were sweetheart stars that only met once every year. "And this is the night they meet, Tammy-*chan*," she'd told me. "I only wish that my sister Yuri and I could meet one day, just like those stars."

Yuri had been mean to our Nana. She had been just as ugly to our Grandpa, who had died six months after Nana because, Mama said sadly, they had loved each other so much they couldn't live without each other.

She really was Mean Yuri! She didn't deserve to have Mama named for her. I went to bed with hate in my heart and fell asleep vowing that tomorrow I'd do everything I could to help Ken with his plan to get us home.

What woke me was the pounding of the sea. The sound was so loud that it seemed as if waves were breaking right against the wall of the house. All I really wanted to do was hide under the covers, but the boom-slosh-boom sounds kept me listening. Like huge fists hammering and smashing, each pound jolted the house, and after a while it seemed as if the ocean was shouting out a song.

"Down deep, down deep," the sea-voices seemed to bellow. "Come deep, down, down. The going is easy, returning is scary, scary..."

I'm not making this up—that was what it sounded like. It was awesome and scary, but mostly scary. I thought of running into Ken's room, but I knew he'd laugh at me, so I stayed where I was.

I guess I fell asleep. The next thing I knew, the sun was shining bright and hot through the one window in my room.

To rile Mean Yuri, Ken had left the bathroom a mess. He'd left the tap running and had thrown towels on the floor and left the soap lying in the middle of the sink. I wondered what he'd done in the kitchen, but when I got there, Yuri was sitting at the table alone, reading the paper and sipping from a mug.

"Japanese tea. Want to taste?" she asked.

It was the color of pee. I said, "No thanks," and went to look for juice and milk.

"There is no milk—your brother spilled it," Yuri said. "You can have dry cereal or bread."

My cue to whine and act like a brat—but there she was sitting looking cool and tough, and I couldn't get up the nerve. So I made myself toast while she went on sipping and reading, and after a while she asked about my plans for the day.

"I am going to paint *pleine aire*—which means, outside on the beach," she explained. "If you wish, you can swim then."

I got up the courage to leave my plate on the table for her to clean up and went to put on my bathing suit and find my flip-flops. Then, ignoring Mean Yuri's orders to take a hat, I ran out into the heat of the porch and down the boardwalk to the beach. This morning the tide was way out. Shells were scattered all over our strip of beach. Ken was poking a stick at a huge jellyfish that had washed up on the shore.

In the daytime the beach was a different place. The frightening sea-noises had changed to a playful roll and splat. I was ashamed I'd been so scared. But there was still something dark about the sea that made me sit down on the sand and wait for Yuri to come down, set up a huge umbrella and her easel, and tell us we were free to swim. "Stay in the shallow water, *ne?*" she ordered, "Or else you will be obliged to come out at once!"

"As if she could make us," Ken scoffed, but we didn't stay around to sass her. We didn't want to keep the ocean waiting.

We swam and splashed all morning until we were too tired to do much more than sprawl at the edge of the sea and let the waves roll over us. We spent a lot of time watching bug-eyed ghost crabs scuttling in and out of their deep, fist-sized burrow holes. Mr. Sol had told us that these white, spindly-legged characters were actually evolving from sea creatures into land creatures. Right now they had to make several dashes a day into the ocean shallows to wet their gills, thus setting themselves up to being eaten by seagulls. But someday they would be able to quit doing this.

I thought ghost crabs were cool, but Mr. Sol had said they bore watching. He'd said that they were a menace to turtles because one of their favorite meals was Hatchlings Tartare. Ken explained that tartare meant raw meat. I got that queasy feeling again. I was going to have to keep my eyes on those ghost crabs!

After a while Ken got busy digging some old hole, while I went looking for shells and ended up near Yuri, who was putting blue-green paint on a big canvas. It didn't look like anything I could put a name to, but somehow it had a feel of the sea. Just looking at that canvas reminded me of the song the sea had seemed to sing last night.

Down deep, down, down deep—

"What's that you are saying?" Yuri asked.

Embarrassed that I'd said the words out loud, I mumbled, "It's a kind of song the sea might sing. If it had a voice, I mean."

She gave me a long look out of those almost-black eyes and said, "Not many can hear the songs of the sea." She drew a single line into the painting, and I suddenly saw the curl of a wave about to break. "Last night their song was strong."

Shocked quiet to know that she understood what I meant, I sat down on the sand and watched her curve another line into the almost-shape of a seagull. "The sea is a mystery," she said, after a little while. "People say the sea is cruel or kind, but that cannot be."

"Why not?"

"The sea is part of *shizen*—nature. Sometimes we are hurt or even killed by the sea, but not maliciously. Nature cannot feel. It just *is*."

I thought of what our new friend, Mr. Sol, had said about that natural selection thing. "Turtles feel, don't they?" I wondered out loud.

She flicked her brush, and drops of white and pale yellow seawater foamed the canvas. "Why do you talk about turtles?" I explained about turtle nest #8, and she gave me a surprised look. "I did not tell you, but I am painting a picture inspired by a famous turtle. Have you heard the tale about *Urashima Taro*?"

Here came one of her goofy stories. I looked over at Ken, but he was busy digging. I could have gotten up and moved, but I was too lazy.

"Once, long ago, there was a poor fisherman," Yuri began. "His name was Urashima Taro. You know that in Japan the surnames are always put first. No? That way, we learn immediately, to which family a person belongs. Anyway, Taro was poor, not because he wasn't a good fisherman but because he was too tenderhearted. If he hooked a fish, he felt sorry for it and more than likely let it go."

I yawned loudly to show how interested I was, but she just went on talking.

"You ask, why didn't Taro give up fishing? Not so easy. Taro's father had been a fisherman, and his grandfather, and his great grandfather, they were all fishermen. So it was expected that Taro would be a fisherman, too. In Japan you have to do what the head of the family tells you to do."

"Always?" She nodded. "But supposing..."

"No 'supposing' about it." Yuri picked up a really ratty looking paintbrush with a blue handle and dipped it in paint. "One day, Taro saw some bad children throwing stones at a small turtle. Taro chased the children away and took the little turtle and put it back in the ocean. 'Swim away safely, my little brother,' he told the turtle."

Yuri's blue-handled brush touched her canvas. Eyes half closed against the dazzling sun, I watched a turtle take shape on the canvas.

Pretty soon, Yuri said, Taro and his parents had nothing more to eat. He went to the beach determined to catch something, and that was when he heard a voice calling him.

I yawned again. "The little turtle, I bet."

"Oh, but the turtle was no longer small and helpless. *Ne?* Now it was a giant turtle with jewels encrusting its shell. 'I came to thank you,' said the turtle, 'and to offer an invitation. Will you come down to the Sea King's palace? He wants to thank you, personally, for your kindness to all the creatures of the sea.'

Yuri's brush was moving quickly now, too quickly for my eyes to follow. But wait... I blinked, for there was the giant turtle with Taro on its back. They were moving down, down, down into the green darkness of the sea.

"Taro had often wondered if there was a world under the sea, so he happily accepted the invitation. 'Sit on my back,' said the turtle, and off they went down to the Sea King's palace, which was wonderful, let me tell you."

Yuri started to describe the palace, but she didn't have to. Her brush was showing me. There it was, the palace made out of mother of pearl with gates made of coral. Brightly colored sea anemones bowed and danced as the giant turtle escorted Taro up to a throne made out of huge pearls.

"The Sea King and the Princess greeted Taro," Yuri said, and the Sea King waved his trident and the princess smiled at Taro. She really was beautiful, with her sea green hair flowing about her. When Taro approached, she stepped down from her throne and held out her hands...

Whoa. I blinked. The figures on Yuri's canvas were actually moving. A trick of the light? I blinked again—hard.

"How..." I began, but Yuri was telling her story.

"It was beautiful under the sea," she continued. "So beautiful that Taro forgot everything and anything except having a good time."

Sure they were. Eating and dancing and playing games with fish that were painted every color of the rainbow. They darted, spiraled, practically leaped out of the canvas at me. I couldn't have looked away even if I'd wanted to.

"But as time passed, Taro became homesick," Yuri said, softly. "The Sea King's palace was beautiful and his own small cottage a poor and uncomfortable place, but it was his home. Also, Taro had begun to miss his family so much that he felt pain in his heart. We all know this feeling, do we not, the missing that hurts?"

Something in her voice made me drag my eyes away from the canvas to look at her and—here was a surprise—because she was watching me with a look that was, well, almost kind.

Why should she want to be kind to me? We hadn't been nice to her ... but I didn't have time to think because the scene on Yuri's canvas was changing again. Guided by Yuri's brush, Taro thanked the Sea King and begged to be taken back to the surface.

The Sea King tried to talk sense to him, Yuri said. "Why do you want to go back to a poor hut and hunger and sorrow? It is your choice, of course, but think about this carefully. Stay with us and we will make you happy and you will never want for anything ever again."

Did Taro listen? No, he did not. Then, Yuri said, the Princess gave Taro a box saying, 'This is a gift from my father. Open it only when you are truly lost and lonely in your own world.'

On Yuri's canvas Taro again sat on the turtle's back, and in his hands was a jeweled box. "The going is easy, the coming back is often frightening," Yuri sighed as the big turtle swam to the surface and let Fisherman Taro off its back. "But—now, home sweet home. Taro wanted nothing more than to go tell his family and friends all about the sea kingdom, and then he wanted a bath and dinner and his own bed. He set off for home, but soon he realized that the road didn't look the same, and all the old landmarks were gone. And as for his little village—where was it? What was this big town doing here?"

Scenes shifted on Yuri's canvas. No more a humble fishing village, Taro's village was now full of handsome homes and gardens and condos. Taro didn't know where he was! At first he thought that the turtle had made a mistake in directions, and so he asked a young man how he could make his way to his village.

I could see how startled the young man was even before Yuri said, "The young man stared, open mouthed. 'But, sir," he stammered, 'that village was destroyed in a fire many years ago. The people built this town instead.'

"Taro became even more confused and blurted, 'But I live in the village! I left it only yesterday. My name is Urashima Taro.'

"Now the young man looked frightened. 'Stranger,' he stammered, 'what are you saying? Taro the fisherman was lost at sea more than sixty years ago. His family was so upset they cried for weeks!' And where was the family now? 'Alas,' said the young man, 'they are all dead and gone.'

"Taro was terribly distressed. He ran through the town asking people about his family and friends. One old lady remembered knowing Urashima Taro, but she was nearly blind and hard of hearing, and she did not recognize our poor young fisherman."

Yuri put down the blue-handled brush and looked thoughtfully at her canvas, which had changed again. No moving turtle, no dancing fish, no Sea King's palace— only swirls of blue and green that made you think of the sea. I rubbed my eyes. Had I imagined everything I'd seen? Had I fallen asleep and dreamed it all? That had to be it.

"So... what happened to Taro?" was all I could think to say.

"Finally Taro realized what had happened. He thought he'd been only down at the bottom of the sea for a few hours, but in truth sixty years had passed! Sadness filled him, and he sat down on the ground and wept for all the loved ones he had lost. Just then, he remembered the Sea King's gift. He drew out the small, precious box and

held it in his hand and wondered if he should open it."
She turned to me, suddenly. "Would you have opened?"

"I guess. Maybe. I don't know."

"Taro did open the box. And out of it rose a soft, white
smoke that swirled around him, and as it did he began
to feel a great weariness, and his bones began to ache.
He raised his hands and saw that they had become wrin-
kled and feeble. He found a puddle of water and looked
into it and saw his face and gasped. Taro had become an
old, old man."

She stopped. "Then what happened?" I asked. She
shook her head. "You mean that's the end of the story?
But—but why couldn't the Sea King have warned Taro
that this was going to happen? Then he could've stayed
under the sea and been happy."

"Is that what you would have done?" I started to nod
but then thought about it. Taro had really missed his
friends and his home and his family.

"Okay," I argued, "so he had to go home. But what
about afterward, when he found out he had no family left?
He could've gone back to the Sea King's palace, right? I'll
bet they'd have taken him back if he'd asked."

"Ah, but he didn't ask." Yuri got up, stretched, and
started to clean her brushes. "I think that once he

realized that his loved ones had gone, it was his choice to die, too."

I thought of Grandpa Louis. "Sometimes," Yuri was saying somberly, "there really is no good choice."

Chapter 7

THAT NIGHT WHEN DAD CALLED, I grabbed the phone before Ken could get his hands on it.

Dad sounded beat down tired as he told me that Mama was about the same. "So, tell me, Littlebit, how do you like all that water?"

Before I could tell him anything, Ken grabbed the phone away and took it to the back of the couch where he crouched and talked in muffled grunts. "Yeah, but, Dad—can't we just—I don't want to stay here all summer, dang it—yes, sir, I guess." Finally, he straightened up and handed the phone to Yuri. "He wants to talk to you."

This was the time for her to tell our dad everything and complain about how we were being brats. We held our breath, hoping to hear Mean Yuri tell Dad about how we'd worn our sandy flip-flops into the house this afternoon grinding the sand into the living room rug, and about how Ken had sassed her when she told him to take the vacuum cleaner out and sweep up that sand. "Don't have to do what you tell me to," he'd said to her, being as ugly as he possibly could be, and I'd chimed in with, "You're not the boss of us."

Now she would tell Dad that she couldn't stand us and was bringing us home. But instead here was Mean Yuri telling Dad about the weather and how we were all enjoying the beach together and getting to know each other. Then she said we'd expect his call tomorrow around this time and hung up the phone.

We couldn't believe it. What was it going to take for Yuri to throw us out? Maybe, I muttered to Ken, it was my fault. I should have just walked off in the middle of her turtle story today, but then the pictures had started to move. I started to tell Ken about that, but he was in a bad mood and told me he didn't want to hear my made-up stories. "You fell asleep and had a dream," was his explanation, and I guessed that it was probably the only explanation that made sense. "What we have to think about is how to get us home," he muttered. "We have to think of something."

He broke off as Yuri cleared her throat and asked us did we want to play cards. Ken just snorted and turned on the TV, but I said, sure. It was maybe a chance to aggravate her.

So I sat down with her at the kitchen table and we played Old Maid except that she called it another name. "Old Miss," she said, her voice husky and without a drop of humor to it.

Here was a perfect opening. "Like you, right?" She nodded. "How come you didn't get married?"

"When I was young, marriage customs were different in Japan." From the look on Mean Yuri's face, she didn't want to go there, no how, no way.

I leaped at the chance. "How different?"

"My father arranged a meeting for me." Short, not wanting to talk about it.

"A meeting with who?"

Yuri sighed and picked up her cards. "A gentleman." I asked how old she was back then. "Fifteen. Are you going to play cards or not?"

To keep things going, I pretended to be interested in playing Old Miss, but I kept prodding. "You didn't like him?" No answer. "I said, didn't you like..."

"I did not like." I noticed that her hands had started to shake.

"So you turned this man down," I persisted.

"I told my father I wanted to study art." Mean Yuri threw down another matched pair. "My father was very angry."

"What did he do?"

"He sent me to my uncle and aunt in Kyoto, and—ha! Look, you are the Old Miss, Tammy!"

I offered to play another game, but she said she had the turtle painting to finish and retreated to her studio. "Good work, you really had her going," Ken grinned, but I wasn't so sure. There'd been something in Yuri's face when she talked about her uncle and aunt that made me wish I hadn't asked.

Ken must have guessed what I was thinking, because he repeated that we had to do whatever it took to get back home. "It's the only way," he said.

I was a little more used to the sea-sounds tonight, but maybe that was because it was low tide. High tide came crashing in the early dawn and woke me while it was still dark.

The clock by my bed said it wasn't even six o'clock yet, but I couldn't sleep any more and even Nana Honey's music box didn't help, so I went out into the hall and saw that I wasn't the only one who couldn't sleep. The light in Mean Yuri's studio was on. Today the door was cracked open, so I peeked in.

Yuri sat in a chair by the still-dark window, sketching. On the desk beside her lay a cup of that weird Japanese tea. Yuri's face was half in shadow, and her long gray hair was loose and hanging around her shoulders. All of her was still except for her hand.

After a while she looked up and saw me watching. "You are up early," she said, abruptly.

It was too early to even start thinking of ways to rile our so-called aunt. I started to back out of the doorway, but then she said, "Do you want to see?"

Gingerly I stepped into the studio. It smelled of oil and turpentine, and there was the turtle painting on the easel. I gave it a suspicious glance, but it was just a painting in blues and greens. Another canvas, white and ready for paint, leaned against the wall. Yuri was a quick worker.

"Are you afraid I will bite you?" she asked. "Come closer and look." She held out her open sketchbook, and I stared at me and Ken prancing into the water. Just a few lines, yet there we were.

"Whoa," I said, surprised that she was so good. "Can I see the rest?"

Wordless, she handed me the book, and I sat down on the floor and looked at sketches of people I didn't recognize, and landscapes, and street scenes. There was a dog curled up, and another dog running. There was also a sketch of an old lady sitting down in a chair and reading a book.

"My mother," Yuri explained.

"You didn't draw her face," I protested.

"It's just a sketch, Tammy." I asked if she had a sketch of her father, too. "No," she said, and then flipped the pages forward again until suddenly there was Ken, arms folded across his chest, glowering at us. A flip of the page and there I was, holding Dad's hand and looking up at him. She'd caught the pleading misery of me so well that I had to look away.

She knew exactly what was going on. Yuri understood the way we felt about being here. Embarrassed but not wanting her to see, I turned to look around her studio. Everything was carefully arranged. Next to me stood her box of brushes, and on top of them all was the old brush with the blue handle. I started to pick it up.

"Leave it alone!" Her voice was sharp, and I pulled my hand away. "Artist's things are best touched only by artist," she went on. "You do not like it when your brother touches your book of stories."

How would she know that? But that 'how' started a whole list of other questions in my mind, uncomfortable questions. I was edging myself out of the studio when she called me back.

"This is for you," she said.

'This' was a small notebook. Not the spiral kind you can buy in a store but one that was covered with pretty Japanese paper. "Have you a pen?" Yuri asked. When I shook my head, she reached into her pocket and pulled out a ballpoint. "To write your stories in," she explained.

I stammered thanks, but already she was bent over her sketchbook. I went back to my room, sat down on my bed and wondered: just who was Yuri Hamada?

The Mean Hag Aunt who'd made Nana Honey cry? The tough lady who'd come out of nowhere and taken Ken and me away from home even though she didn't have a clue about kids? The woman we hated?

She was all of those things, but she was also the one who'd heard the songs of the sea. She was the storyteller who'd remembered that I liked to write stories, too. She was a painter who could make a canvas come alive and tell a story... I let that thought drift away. I couldn't possibly have seen what I'd seen yesterday.

Chapter 8

THE LITTLE NOTEBOOK in my hand could be a bribe. Or not. It was confusing, and I hated the feeling, so I pulled on my shorts and a top and got a bowl of cereal, which I took out on the deck. The sun was just starting to poke out of the sea, and after a while the pelican family came flying by. Mama would have loved watching those birds.

Mama is sitting next to me on the rocker, shading her eyes with her hand. As usual, she's forgotten her sunhat, and her hair tickles my cheek. We're eating chocolate chip ice cream, and I've just read her something I'd written...

The daydream snapped as Ken came out onto the porch and walked past me down the boardwalk.

I followed. "Want to go check the turtle nest?" I asked. He shrugged. "Maybe the turtles hatched."

"They won't hatch for weeks." Ken spoke as if he had something on his mind, so I just walked along without talking.

"She's going to paint on the beach..." he finally said.

"She's a good artist," I added. Half expecting him to make some mean remark, I was surprised when he just shrugged again.

I followed, and we walked along without talking until Ken burst out, "I'm sick of being lied to."

"What's the matter with you?" I asked.

Ken was chewing on his lower lip. "She talks and talks about how important family is, but she didn't even *think* to write Nana Honey or Mama!"

"She didn't get Nana's letters, so she didn't have her address," I pointed out. Ken gave me a strange look.

"Yes, she did." He pulled something out of his pocket and shoved it under my nose. "Look at this."

'This' was a letter, written on thin, pale green paper that I recognized as Nana Honey's favorite rice paper stationary. "Where'd you get this?"

"Just read it," Ken snapped.

I unfolded the letter and read Nana's careful English telling her dear little sister that she had a granddaughter.

"'And a grandson, Kenjiro,'" I read aloud and repeated, "Where did you get this?"

"Yuri's studio." Ken's eyebrows were pulled together in a dark frown. "I snuck in there while she was in the shower and looked in the desk drawer. There was a kind of scrapbook in there with stuff..." His voice rose. "I *knew* she wasn't telling the truth about Nana's letters, and here's the proof. She knew all the time about Nana Honey. Yuri wanted her dead—like her father."

I felt a little sick. "You've got to put that back, Ken. If she finds out you took it..."

"He-ey!"

Mr. Sol was waving to us down the beach. Ken snatched the letter from me and shoved it back into his pocket. "I'll put it back," he promised. "I want to go back in that studio of hers, anyway. See what else she's been lying about."

He raced over to Mr. Sol. I followed in time to hear our friend say, "No activity in nest #8. You're up early," he added. "Maybe you could give me a hand hauling my stuff down from the house."

His "stuff" included a tripod, a backpack full of camera equipment, and an expensive-looking camera. Mr. Sol carried that himself, and Ken carried the tripod and the backpack. Seeing that I might feel left out, Mr. Sol handed me a folding stool and said that this was the most important part of the whole she-bang.

"Sometimes a photographer has to sit tight to take his best shots," was the way he put it.

As we three walked slowly down to the beach, Mr. Sol explained that he'd been up since five photographing the sky. "Incredible colors," he enthused. "Now, I want to catch the way light changes on the water."

After we got Mr. Sol to the spot he wanted, Ken ran back for a water bottle. Then I ran to get the Boston Red Sox hat. "You're going to run your legs off being my gofer," he said when we'd come panting back to him. "I'm going to have to hire you."

Ken said we'd be glad to help out anytime.

"I'm talking about regular employment here," Mr. Sol said. "I need somebody with legs to do some back-and-forthing for me. You two interested in a part-time job?"

We were shaking over a deal of ten dollars a day when Yuri came walking toward us.

"I am Yuri Hamada," she said to our friend. "Aunt to these children." And while he tipped his cap and introduced himself, she gave him the coolest look-over I'd ever seen. "You are the man who watches turtles, also a photographer?"

Mr. Sol said he'd been taking photographs all his life. "All summer I try to get to know the effect of early sunlight on sky and water," he added.

Yuri sighed. "I have tried for forty five years, but still the light is hard to capture."

"There are surprises all the time. I've stayed on Emerald Isle for three summers, now, but the light—don't you find that at dawn the sky..."

"...Changes constantly? Yes! The smallest variation, sound, even taste make differences, *ne?*"

They stood there smiling at each other. "Do you need us any more, Mr. Sol?" Ken asked, a little too loudly.

"No, not now. Check back in a few hours. I'm going to the library later, if you two want to come along." Then Mr. Sol went back to talking to Mean Yuri.

We walked away, feeling ignored and baffled. Who would want to be friends with Yuri? "While they're talking we can get the letter back into the studio," Ken said.

"*We?*"

He shot me a scornful look. "You going to wimp out on me, Tam?"

I knew that it was our chance to find out what else Mean Yuri was hiding, but I felt queasy as we opened her studio door and stepped inside. Everything was the same as it had been this morning with Yuri's brushes, paints, and sketchbooks neatly in their places. I was about to tell Ken to hurry up so that we could get out of there when a movement in the corner of the room caught my eye. I looked over, quick, and *thought* I saw a turtle swimming across Yuri's painted canvas.

"Look at this, Tam..." Ken was standing near the desk. He was holding a scrapbook and was rifling through it. "There's newspaper clippings and everything. This one's from the *London Times*. I guess Yuri had an exhibition in London."

Keeping a watchful eye on Yuri's turtle canvas, I listened as Ken read from the clipping in his hand. It praised Yuri Hamada's paintings and wondered how such a young artist could convey such depths in her art. "'Hamada has an almost magical way of drawing onlook- ers into her paintings,'" Ken was reading out loud. "'If one were fanciful, one might believe the stories about her famous teacher, Asuka Kawana, who reportedly studied the ancient art of *Onmyodo*. Even today some believe that an *Onmyoji* can call upon the ancient spirits of earth, sea and sky...'"

Footsteps on the boardwalk! "She's coming," I hissed. Quickly, Ken pushed the scrapbook back into the desk drawer and closed it. I was already out of the studio door and making tracks for my room when he joined me.

"I don't care how many nice things they say about her," he growled. "We've got to get home, Tam. I don't think Dad's telling us everything. He sounded really whipped."

"Of course he was whipped. He always is. Not telling us about what?"

Ken said he couldn't put his finger on it. "Something about Mama's bugging him. Extra, I mean. I thought about it all night, Tam. I hope Mama's not worse."

How much worse could it get? I wanted to cry, but I knew there were worse things, things I didn't even want to put names to.

I wished Ken had kept his 'feelings' to himself. It made me jumpy. Later, I snapped at something Ken said, and then we had this huge fight with both of us yelling. Then I pushed Ken, and he threatened to smack me, and Mean Yuri got between us and shouted for us to stop.

"I will not have ugly yellings," she lectured us. "Brother and sister should take care of each other, not fight."

"Like you and *your* sister?" Ken snapped back. Her eyes narrowed to black slits, and for a second I really thought she was going to haul off and smack him. But all she did was send us to our rooms.

We were only allowed out to eat Yuri's awful stew, which tasted like boiled rubber, and later we got to talk to Dad on the phone. Then it was, "Back into your rooms, and no nonsenses!" Yuri ordered us. Ken took his revenge by singing rap with insulting words aimed at Yuri, but I just sat on my bed and sulked until I was tired enough to fall asleep.

And then I dreamed of Mama. At least, I think it was a dream.

I dreamed that I was riding out to sea on the back of a big turtle. At first the sea was calm and blue and it was fun to be out there on the turtle's back. But then there was a wind like a hurricane pushing and pushing me off the turtle's back, and I fell into the cold water.

Deep, down deep I fell, and then suddenly my turtle swam by, only now Mama was sitting on its back. She blew me a kiss goodbye, and I knew she was going down to the Sea King's palace and would never come back to us again.

I called her name over and over, but she had disappeared. I was crying my heart out when, suddenly, I felt her arms around me. Mama was holding me, and I heard her singing her song to me.

"The going is easy, coming back is scary..."

This is the part I'm not sure was a dream because I could really feel her arms holding me, and I even heard her talking to me.

"Shh, hush," I heard Mama say. "It's all right, Tammy. It was just a nightmare."

Then she started to sing again, and I knew Ken was wrong and Mama was all right. She wasn't under the ocean with the Sea King. She was right here with me, and we were both safe, so I could go to sleep again and not be afraid any more.

Chapter 9

THE FIRST THING I DID when I woke up the next morning was to write about my dream. It was better than any story I could have thought up, and when I played Nana Honey's music box like I did every morning, I found that I could actually remember some of the words to Mama's song. I was trying to remember more of the words when Yuri tapped on my door and asked if I wanted breakfast.

When she saw that I was using the notebook she'd given me, she looked pleased and asked what story I was writing. I didn't want to tell her about my dream, so I just shrugged.

"Quite right," she said, and flashed her brief, rare smile. "Artists should never discuss a work in progress. I am going down to the beach to paint like Ikkyu-san, so you can come down and swim if you like."

Ken had already gone off to help Mr. Sol. I guessed he was still mad at me because he hadn't got me up to come, too. That was okay by me because I wanted to finish my dream-story. It was a while before I changed into my bathing suit and flip-flops, and by the time I got down to the beach, Yuri was slapping paint onto her canvas.

"Your brother has gone down to help Sol-san," she informed me. "I thought you were both employed by him."

No smile, now—she was narrow-eyed with concentration. She wanted me out of her hair, which was my cue to start bugging her. Innocently, I asked, "Who's Ikkyu-san?"

"Nobody that would interest you. Why not go and see how you can earn your pocket money?"

Never mind that I was still mad at him, Ken would've been proud of the way I plunked myself down on the sand. "Is Ikkyu-san a story?" No answer. "You like to tell stories," I reminded her. "You told the one about Fisherman Taro and that gross one about the bee..."

Very slowly, Yuri put down her brush. "Go away and stop bothering me."

Her eyes were black as stones and her voice had a steely edge. Pretty scary. I would have gladly left her, but here was my chance to do some serious damage! So I pulled in a deep breath and gave her the sweetest smile I could manage. "Who was Ikkyu-san?"

She said a whole lot of Japanese words, which trust me, couldn't have been nice ones. Then she said, "If I tell you this story, will you promise to go away and leave me to paint in peace?" I nodded. "Then be quiet and listen."

Sweet as sugar, I folded my hands in my lap and pretended to listen as Yuri picked up her ratty old brush with the blue handle. She dabbed a little paint on the canvas and began, "A long time ago there lived a little Japanese boy, and there is a legend about him. When he was still a little child, he entered a temple to become an acolyte."

"What's an ac—whatever?"

"An apprentice. A helper. Do you want to hear the story or do you mean to interrupt me every other minute? Later he was given another name, but for now we will call the boy Little Kyu. Now, Little Kyu was homesick and hated the temple, which was old and dark and full of noises, especially at night. He was afraid of the Chief Abbot who was a big man with a large, round stomach and a voice like a bull. The abbot was proud and impatient and didn't like small boys, and all the other monks ignored Little Kyu, also. His only friend was the abbot's cat."

"What was the cat's name?" She gave me a dirty look. "Well, you can't call him Cat all the time," I pointed out, "You could call him Buttons, or Morris, maybe."

"Tama was his name," said Yuri. Then, she added, "Sounds like your name, ha? *Tama* means 'ball' in Japanese."

I hadn't known that, and I was going to make sure Ken didn't find out, either, or he'd make jokes about my silly name 'til he turned blue. I was frowning over this when Tama appeared on Yuri's canvas. I'm not kidding, he *arrived*. One second there was nothing on the canvas and then there he was, a small, fat, white cat with tawny ears and a bell around his neck. Then, while I was staring, Tama meowed at me.

So help me! You can believe me or not, but that painted feline opened its painted mouth and meowed at me.

Yuri went on, "Tama was the little boy's only friend and followed after him while Little Kyu drew water from the creaky old well, or washed the long, wooden hallway, or studied long and boring lessons. Kyu always gave Tama a little bit of his own poor supper, and Tama was the only one who saw Kyu drawing, which was something he loved more than anything in life. He'd take a bit of charcoal and sketch animals and people and houses on the flagstones before he washed them clean. He'd find a stick and draw angels of heaven and wild and terrible ogres in the temple sand."

And—there, springing from the blue-handled brush was Little Kyu, shaven-headed and too small for his robes, drawing with a stick in the temple courtyard. His fist was all grubby, and there was a streak of soot on his face.

"He's so little," I breathed.

"Yes. Always hungry, usually cold. But if he could draw..." Yuri's brush created a bird, "then, he was free."

"How do you do that?" I cried as the bird fluttered away.

"Do what? Pay attention to the story!" Yuri started to touch more paint to her canvas. "One day," she said, "the Abbot caught Kyu drawing and became very angry. 'We must teach you a lesson,' he bellowed, and then he commanded that Kyu be taken into the dark, gloomy temple and tied to the stout center pillar. 'See how you like staying here all night,' he told the little boy. 'In the morning you must promise never to draw again, and then you will be freed.' Then off he went. And he took Tama with him, too."

"You mean, Little Kyu had to be tied up all night?" I cried. "That's so mean!"

"The Abbott didn't really do this to be mean," Yuri explained. "He wanted to cure the boy of what he thought was a useless habit. The Abbot, who thought himself a very wise man, was sure he knew what was good for the little boy. Of course, Kyu cried all night."

Aunt Yuri's lips tightened, and she took a gob of paint and splashed it hard onto the canvas, and the gob became a small, scared, hunched figure shaking with sobs. "It was cruel, *ne*? Kyu loved to draw. It was like the breathing of air to her. How could she ever give up painting? How *could* she? But they wouldn't listen even when she cried and cried..."

I stared at Aunt Yuri. "But—but I thought Kyu was a boy!"

"He is. Stop interrupting. Do you want to hear the story or not?" Yuri took a deep breath and began to smooth out the blob she had made. "In the morning the temple was very still," she went on. "The Abbot and all the monks went to see how Kyu had fared during the night. They were convinced that the scared boy would swear never to paint another picture. Together with them came Tama, who had waited all night to be with his little friend! Suddenly, the cat began to growl, and his fur stood on end, and he stared hard at a mouse on the ground beside Kyu's feet. 'A rat! Go get it!' shouted the Abbot.

"The cat pounced—but there was no rat. There had never been a rat. Looking closer, the Abbot saw that Kyu had dipped his toe in his own tears and painted a mouse on the floor. The painting had been so good that even Tama was fooled."

"Did the Abbot take a fit?"

"Probably. But then he also realized that Kyu was a talented artist. And because at heart he wasn't a bad man, the Abbot decided to let Kyu paint as much as he wanted from that day on. And he did paint—wonderful scrolls and great paintings which are hung in the temple to this day."

"Then it's a real story?" Forgetting that my mission in life was to irritate Mean Yuri, I cried, "All that about the mouse is true?"

"It's just a legend, Tammy..." but before Yuri could say more we heard shouting in the distance.

"That's Ken's voice," I exclaimed.

Could be he was in trouble—never mind that I was still mad at him, I jumped to my feet and took off down the beach, running hard until I could see small figures grouped around turtle nest #8. Mr. Sol was there, and Mrs. Cora Fowler, who was pointing at Ken and screaming.

"He did it, he did!" The wind carried Halsey's voice toward me, and there was the gum-popper himself sitting on the boardwalk steps. I wasn't near enough to see his face, but I could bet it was set in meanness. "He took it, Grandma," Halsey was yelping. "I saw him going over to your car..."

"You're a lying twerp, Halsey." As I ran up to the group, Ken added, "I wasn't anywhere near that car. I was doing stuff for Mr. Sol."

"Which means you were near my house," Mrs. Fowler interrupted. "You saw my car door open, didn't you? Saw my purse on the seat. You saw your chance to steal."

I tugged at Mr. Sol's arm and asked what was going on. "Mrs. Fowler has accused Ken of stealing her wallet," Mr. Sol said, grimly.

Her face almost as red as her hair, Mrs. Fowler said that she'd known all along that Ken wasn't to be trusted. "Now, look," Mr. Sol said, "this is foolish. I've kept Ken running all morning. He didn't have time to sneeze let alone sneak around to steal your purse."

Halsey unwrapped a new piece of purple bubble gum and popped it into his mouth. "Grandma, he did take it," he whined. "I saw him do it."

"Then you are mistaken," a voice said behind us, and there was Yuri Hamada, her blue-handled paintbrush still clasped in her hand, her sunhat jammed down on her head. "Ken did not take your wallet," she said.

"And who may you be?" Mrs. Fowler looked Yuri up and down so hatefully that I itched to smack her.

"I am Ken's aunt, Yuri Hamada." Calmly, she gave Mrs. Fowler look for look. "You are mistaken," she repeated. "My nephew does not steal."

Mrs. Fowler snorted and then switched her gaze to Mr. Sol. "I blame you, Mr. Knitsbridge. If you hadn't trusted this—this juvenile delinquent, this wouldn't have happened." She said a lot more, but I wasn't paying attention. I was looking at Halsey, who was enjoying himself to no end. When he saw me looking, he stuck his tongue out at me.

Oh, he was going to get it—but Mr. Sol put his hand on my shoulder, pulling me back. "Ken, let's see what you have in your pockets, son."

Ken dug his hands in his pockets, turned them upside down. "Doesn't mean anything—he could have ditched the wallet in the bushes," Rat Halsey squeaked.

"Did you see Ken take this wallet, or is that what you wish you saw?" Yuri demanded. She held Halsey's eyes with her own until he looked away. Then she said, "Let me hear what happened—from the beginning."

"What happened was that this boy..."

"From the beginning, please."

Yuri stared directly at Mrs. Fowler, who'd started to turn pale with anger, and waited. Finally, the red-headed lady muttered that she'd gone out to her car to go to the supermarket, but then the phone had rung inside the house.

"I went inside to answer the phone leaving my purse in the car. It was right in my car, in full view. When I came out, my wallet was gone."

Yuri turned to Ken, who said, "I don't know anything about it." He sounded mad and a little scared.

"Let's go up to your car and see what is going on," Yuri then said. She turned to look at Mrs. Fowler again. "We will see what the truth is."

Mrs. Fowler squinched her mean old eyes to disagree, but Mr. Sol was already heading up the steps in front of Yuri. Ken and I ran after him, and Mrs. Fowler followed with Halsey.

Yuri was waiting for us at the top of the steps. She nodded toward a green car in the next driveway. "Your car?" she asked Mrs. Fowler.

The redheaded lady said, shortly, that it was, and Yuri walked toward the car. "The driver's side door is open. Is this how you left it?" Mrs. Fowler nodded. "Did you look to see if your wallet fell onto the floor?"

"Of course I did." Face scrunched in scorn, Mrs. Fowler stomped up to the car, and lifted her purse from the front seat. Gaped it wide to show the contents. Then, bending down, she ran her red-nailed hand up and down the floor. "Do *you* see a wallet?"

Oh, she was hateful! Yuri asked, "Perhaps you took it into the house with you when you answered the telephone call? Sometimes," she added, "I do things so automatically that I forget I did them."

"My memory is just fine, thank you! What I remember is that this boy—your nephew, you said?—was hanging around Sol's porch when I went into the house. He saw his chance, didn't he? I've always said that you people weren't to be trusted."

"And what people might that be?" Aunt Yuri asked, cool as running water, and polite enough to kill. Mrs. Fowler didn't say anything. "Let us go inside your house and look."

"Good idea. You made an accusation, and you'd better be prepared to back it up," Mr. Sol said before Mrs. Fowler could protest.

"Oh, very well." Off she flounced with Mr. Sol stumping behind her. Yuri stayed back.

"I didn't take anything," Ken started to say in a low voice, but she stopped him.

"Of course not," she said, sounding so certain that Ken flushed up from his neck to his hairline. She glared at Halsey, who'd retreated to the swing on his grandmother's porch. "I don't want you associating with this boy."

"Don't worry," I was beginning, when there was a shout of triumph from Mr. Sol. A few seconds later, he came shambling to the door waving something in his hand.

"You were right, Miss Yuri," he exclaimed. "She brought the wallet inside the house and left it by the telephone, then covered it up with a mess of papers. Mrs. Fowler has some apologizing to do."

White faced and grim-mouthed, Mrs. Fowler stepped out on her porch. Not looking at anybody, she grudged, "It was a misunderstanding,"

"One that will not happen again," Yuri said. I loved the way she sounded—so cool and full of the dignity she'd never lost while Mrs. Fowler was saying ugly things. I admired the way she continued to hold the red-haired lady with her eyes until Mrs. Fowler nodded. Then Yuri added, "Your grandson also must apologize."

But Halsey was nowhere to be seen. "So," Yuri said. "Ken, Tammy, it is time to go."

She turned on her heel and marched down the steps. Ken and I waited for Mr. Sol, who pursed his lips as if making a soundless whistle. "I'll tell you something," he said, soft so only the three of us could hear, "I wouldn't go up against your aunt in court or out. She is one tough lady."

But I was still mad. "Did you see how that Mrs. Fowler looked at her?" I asked Ken. "She acted like Yuri was some kind of trash. And that Halsey! He is so downright mean—I wished I could have smacked him!"

Mr. Sol adjusted his cap thoughtfully. "Sometimes kids get mean from what's done *to* them," he said. "I'm wondering what his family's like."

If they were anything like Mrs. Fowler, Mr. Sol might have a point. But I still wanted to smack that boy.

"Yuri sure took care of them, anyway." Ken started a slow grin, which faded into a puzzled frown. "The way she talked and acted—and she knew just what that lady did with her old wallet, too." Then, as we watched Yuri marching back down the beach toward her easel, he burst out, "What she did to Nana was wrong and all. But still— you have to admit, Tam, that Yuri's kind of cool."

Chapter 10

THAT EVENING, there was a surprise. The UPS man brought a box to the house, and it was from our dad. We tore it open. Dad had put in the new book from a series Ken was crazy about, and a new pair of jeans for me, a kite, and a box of cookies from Mrs. Lauria, our sitter, and a huge book about loggerhead turtles with my name written on it. There were also letters for each of us and a longer one for Yuri. She read it with her eyebrows pulled together in a small frown and then put it into her pocket.

"So you'll know I kind of miss you," Dad said that evening, when we thanked him. "And I sort of remember you. Ah—what were your names again?" We laughed with him glad that tonight he didn't sound worried. "She had a good day," he added, when I asked about Mama. "She looked rested, Littlebit. I think she looked better."

Dad's phone call set us in a happy mood so that we totally forgot to try and rile Yuri. She must have picked up on this because she called on Ken to slice up the watermelon she'd bought from the supermarket. If you asked me, it was kind of pitiful, but Yuri thought it was huge. In Japan, she said, watermelons were small and round and cute.

"How can a watermelon be cute?" Ken lifted his knife, gave a wild yell, and brought the knife smack dab in the middle of the melon. Red juice spurted everywhere.

"Well done. The enemy is defeated." Yuri took one of the halves away and wrapped it in plastic. "Too much for us to eat—I should have asked Sol-san to come share this with us. I would phone him, but I don't know the number."

Ken offered to run over to Mr. Sol's and invite him. While we were waiting, Yuri sliced the remaining watermelon half into bite-sized pieces. "You know Sol-san is a photographer?" she asked me. Of course I knew, I said. "No, a professional. He has gone on shoots for all the big magazines. His work has been exhibited internationally."

Since she seemed to know so much about Mr. Sol, I asked if she knew what had happened to his leg.

"Too sad. A plane crashed in India. For a long time, he told me, he did not know if he would ever walk again." Yuri arranged the fruit on a dish and looked at it critically. "He was in the hospital for months, just like your mother."

Only, Mr. Sol had been able to leave the hospital. He could walk down to the ocean and take photographs of the sun rising while Mama...

"Tammy," Yuri said, interrupting my thoughts, "Do not give up. People who have been in a coma for six months or more have suddenly come awake."

There was the noise of a car engine outside, and then car doors slammed. I ran to the door, and there was Mr. Sol getting out of a van. Ken hopped out the other side. "Thought wheels would be quicker than feet," Mr. Sol said. "Evening, Tammy. Miss Yuri, I'm hoping you haven't forgotten your promise to show me your studio."

Mr. Sol was really impressed with the turtle canvas, even though it wasn't moving. "You've really caught the feel of the sea," he said.

Then Yuri went into a long explanation. It seems that she'd got this idea of combining paintings of the earth, sea and sky with Japanese folktales. This folktale series was what she was working on now.

That sounded pretty clear to me—but adults are weird. They talked and talked about Yuri's project 'til Ken rolled his eyes at me and we went out onto the deck to wait for them to finish.

It was getting dark, and stars were slowly brightening. "Tam," Ken said, suddenly, "remember how bright the stars were when we went camping? We took our sleeping bags out of the tent..."

"And Mama told us to wish on the falling stars. You wished you could make the soccer team at school."

Ken shifted slightly. "Mama was always doing stuff like that. One time— remember, Tam? —when we were little it rained and we couldn't go out to play, she got us to pretend we were stranded on a desert island surrounded by water. Me and you were shipwrecked sailors, and she was this goofy pirate who kept trying to sneak off with our lunch..."

"She used to read my stories like they were important. She thought whatever we did was important." I broke off. "Ken, do you think she'll ever wake up?"

In the dim light I saw that he was frowning. "I'm thinking Dad wrote more to Yuri than he told us."

Just then Yuri and Mr. Sol came out on the deck, still talking about some problem she had with an idea of hers.

"The Celestial Maiden is such an important story," she was saying. "*Ne?* But I cannot find the right inspiration to begin. I have thought and sketched, but I can't see my way."

Mr. Sol nodded sympathetically and said that he understood. "Inspiration can be a tricky thing," he said. "Maybe you need a change in scenery. Come for lunch tomorrow, Miss Yuri, and I'll show you photographs that might spark some ideas. And you two," he added, grinning at us, "get to see some of the ugliest sharks known to man."

After Mr. Sol had gone home, Ken volunteered us to clean up. Yuri gave him a quick look and then said, "Thank you, Ken, that is very thoughtful." Then she added, "I'm glad Mr. Sol came to visit us tonight."

"Yeah." Ken lifted dishes into the sink before he added, "He's a good friend. I mean, he stood up for me this morning with that Mrs. Fowler. And—and I want to thank you, too, Aunt Yuri."

It was the first time he'd called her that. I don't think he even meant to, it sort of slipped out. It surprised Yuri, too, because I saw the tiny quiver that lifted her dark, flaring eyebrows. "Why, thanks? You did not steal. And anyway, I know what it is like to be accused unjustly."

"How do you know?" I asked.

"It happened so many years ago," she said. Then, because we were both looking at her, she added, "I was accused of stealing a rice ball." A what? "*Onigiri,* a rolled up ball made of rice. I was hungry, always wanting food. And when the cook accused me, it seemed logical to her, I suppose."

"But you hadn't taken it, had you?"

"No, but that didn't matter. The cook sent the youngest maid out to cut down a bamboo about three quarters of an inch in diameter. I was beaten," Aunt Yuri said, softly, "beaten and beaten because I wouldn't cry out and because I wouldn't confess."

"That totally sucks," Ken growled. "Did they ever find who did it?" She shook her head. "Didn't you tell your mother about it?"

Instead of answering, Aunt Yuri gave a huge yawn. "I'm very tired," she said. "It's late. I'm going to bed."

She told us to lock the door after us and went. "That's something," Ken mused. "They beat her, and she didn't cry and she didn't confess to something she didn't do. I bet they beat her more than that one time. I bet she didn't cry. She's tough."

I knew different, though. That story of Little Kyu might be a legend, but it was Yuri's story, too. I knew that she had cried at night, alone, when no one could hear her.

"You know something?" Ken was saying. "I'll bet I know where she got beat for something she didn't do. Tam, remember her saying that her parents sent her to her uncle's house? That's where they beat her for eating that rice ball.

Chapter 11

MR. SOL'S HOUSE WAS AWESOME. Smaller and more compact than Yuri's, it had no TV and not much furniture. What it had were photographs. Framed, unframed, mounted and loose, stacked against the walls or all over the chairs and table. Wherever there was space, there was a photograph, even in the bathroom.

You could spend days looking at the photographs, which were of animals and fish and places and nature and people and rocks. Some were in black and white, some in color. Yuri walked around with a look on her face that said she was sure she'd died and gone to heaven. Sol just stood around real quiet but ready to explain anything if a question was asked.

"You are really good," Ken kept saying. "Look at this, Tammy—check it out! And will you look at this shark! What are you going to do with all these, Mr. Sol?"

"That's what I'm trying to decide." Mr. Sol explained that his agent wanted him to have a series of exhibitions, but there was also a publishing house that wanted him to do a book, and a TV station that was after photographs for a documentary. "I've dragged all of this stuff out," he went on, "and I'm going to have to make a decision, but since it's going to take me a few months, I vote we eat lunch first."

"How long did it take you to take all those photos?" I asked as I helped Ken carry plates of sandwiches and a pitcher of sweet tea onto the porch where a big beach umbrella shaded a table set for four. He thought about it and said maybe thirty years.

"And you haven't seen all my slides," he added.

Meanwhile, Aunt Yuri was wandering from room to room, her forehead puckered up and intent, now and then leaning close to look at something in the photo. "You must have the third eye," she called.

Huh? I looked at Ken, who shrugged. Mr. Sol sure looked happy, though, so I guessed it was some kind of weird compliment. He stumped back into the house to talk with Yuri, and Ken said, "Mr. Sol's been teaching me about loggerhead turtles. He says that in the Southeast most of the turtles lay their eggs in Florida, some in South Carolina, some in Georgia. Guess how many of the nests are in North Carolina..."

Feeling put out that Mr. Sol hadn't shared this information with me, I just shrugged and wished I'd read the book that Dad had sent me. "One percent!" Ken said, as smug as if the whole thing was his idea. "Can you beat that? And right near us is nest #8. That makes it sort of special."

It *was* special. Standing on tiptoe at the edge of the porch, I could just see the tips of the wooden structure that enclosed the precious nest. "How many eggs are in that nest, do you think?" I asked.

Ken guessed that there were over a hundred eggs, probably. "Not that they'll all hatch, but still, that's a lot."

"But why doesn't the mother turtle stay with her eggs? She should protect her kids, shouldn't she? A lot more would be born that way."

Ken shrugged and said that was just the way it was. "Don't ask stupid questions," he added. I didn't think it was stupid.

"You know, Tam," Ken continued, lowering his voice as if to tell a secret. "While you've been watching Yuri paint, Mr. Sol's been teaching me about photography. When

I get back to school I'm going to maybe join the camera club, study on being a photo journalist."

"Like you could," I scoffed.

Ken looked down his nose at me so that he looked squint-eyed. "You're just jealous Mr. Sol didn't teach *you!*"

My retort was cut short by the scree-squawk of a porch swing. There was Halsey Fowler glaring at us from his grandma's house and blowing purple bubbles. When he saw us watching, Halsey stuck out his tongue and crossed his eyes and chanted in his squealy voice, "Ugly! Your aunty is so ugly and fat she wears an elephant's panties!"

Ken seethed. "Want me to come over there and show you ugly?"

Halsey jumped up from his swing, shot us the finger, then scuttled into the house and slammed the door. "I'll get that little rat if it takes me all summer," Ken sputtered.

I was getting ready to agree when we heard Yuri protesting loudly. We trooped back into the house to find her holding one of the framed photographs in her hands.

"No, I won't hear of it," Aunt Yuri was exclaiming. "You are too generous, Sol-san, much too generous. No, no.

I must pay or I will have to put this back on the wall and it will break my heart."

"Now, why did you have to say that?" Mr. Sol was trying to frown but smiling instead. He turned to us. "Your aunt is as stubborn as a mule. I want to give her a gift, but she keeps on insisting she wants to pay for it."

"It is you who is resembling a mule," Aunt Yuri scolded, but she was smiling, too. "If I do not pay, I will feel obligated to you, and it will spoil our friendship."

I peeked over her arm at the photograph. It was one I'd never seen before. "Whoa," Ken exclaimed, impressed, "a jellyfish!"

"Not just any jellyfish, pal. It's called a Sea Butterfly," Mr. Sol corrected. "I photographed this beauty as part of a book about *Cnidaria*."

Jellyfish on the shore looked like blobs of Jell-O.™ This one seemed to be airborne, on transparent wings. "The Celestial Maiden," Aunt Yuri breathed. "There she is, the essence of the folk-tale. I have been searching for this inspiration for so long. Sol-san, my dear friend, this picture is beyond price to me."

I stared at our usually stern aunt. Never mind her gray hair, she looked young and almost pretty. Her eyes were bright, and she was smiling as if she was looking at something that only she could see. "But," she went on, "I pay—or I can't accept."

"Give him something you painted in exchange," Ken suggested.

Mr. Sol clapped his hands together and said that was the best idea he'd heard since digital cameras came on the market. "A small sketch, Miss Yuri, how about it? Let's shake on it, and we can eat."

"Yeah, let's," I agreed, and Yuri laughed and held out her slim hand.

"But not a small sketch, a watercolor, perhaps," she added. Mr. Sol said he'd look forward to that. We headed back out to the porch and sat under the big umbrella, and Mr. Sol began to pour the sweet tea. Then he stopped, frowning.

"What's this?"

Lying on the bottom of the pitcher were several lumps. Mr. Sol scooped one up with a spoon.

"Eee-eww!" I gagged.

"What is it?" Yuri asked. "Mud?"

"Bubblegum. Purple bubblegum!" Ken yelped. "Halsey snuck up here while we were—wait 'til I get my hands on that rat weasel!"

He was halfway down the stairs, with me just a step behind him, before Mr. Sol came to the top of the stairs and hollered at us both to come back. "Don't do it," he added. "Halsey's probably hoping you'll jump on him so that he can run to his grandma. It's no big deal. We'll just toss this stuff out and make more tea, that's all."

"But it's not right!" Like me, Ken was itching to rub Weasel Halsey's face into the dirt.

"Well, look at it this way," Mr. Sol said. "Your aunt made Halsey feel pretty small yesterday, and I'm thinking that he's not the kind to forgive and forget. Hopefully, he's got revenge out of his system with this bubblegum caper." Then, as Ken began to sputter that he could make sure of *that* in a hurry, Mr. Sol added softly, "Son, if you're going to make it in this world, you have to learn to pick your battles. Or you'll lose the war."

Chapter 12

BECAUSE I WANTED TO KNOW more about 'our' turtles (and, yes, because I didn't want to sound ignorant the next time Ken bragged about what Mr. Sol was telling him), I read the book Dad sent me from cover to cover. There was something I really wanted to know, and that was how to take care of those turtles, especially the weak ones.

The book was really interesting. I learned a lot more about loggerhead turtles. I found out that they'd got their name because they had such big heads and that they had jaws so strong that they could chomp up crabs and mollusks and those weird creatures that stick to rocks and reefs.

It was pretty unbelievable that a hatchling just two inches could grow into an adult three feet long and weighing between 200 and 350 pounds. I guess that it was OK for turtle mothers to leave their eggs to hatch by themselves on the shore, but they still needed watching. I was going to make sure that all the baby turtles in our turtle nest #8 made it.

Mr. Sol drove Ken and me to the library one day. I loaded up on more books about loggerheads. Then Yuri took us both to the Aquarium at Pine Knoll Shores where a volunteer showed us what the insides of a nest looked like. After that, when I checked up on turtle nest #8, I pictured the tiny babies curled up in their shells, down inside their nest. Yuri said that we might even get to visit a Sea Turtle Hospital, if we had time.

One afternoon when Ken was helping Mr. Sol do a photo shoot and I was alone with the nest, I had an idea. Sitting down in the sand, I sang Mama's song. I figured it was like the lullaby Mom Turtle would have sung to her babies if she had a voice.

"Ooh, isn't that *sweet*."

In mid song I spun around and saw Halsey. He'd snuck up so quietly that I hadn't heard him and was standing right behind me. Seeing that he had my attention, he spat a purple bubble gum right at turtle nest #8.

"Hey, cut that out!" I called, kicking the gum away from the nest.

Halsey sneered. "Gonna make me, Runt?"

Now that Ken wasn't around, Halsey was really acting brave. "I'll bet your grandma would like to know what you were just doing," I told him.

"You mean, when I tell her what I saw *you* doing," he snapped back and popped a purple bubble, which dribbled down his chin "Ooh, she'll really freak when I tell her you were poking holes into her precious old turtle nest."

I looked around but Mr. Sol was sitting in his chair far off down the beach. Ken was back at Yuri's beach. I could holler and scream, and they'd never hear me. I said, "You're a liar and a rat weasel," which made him laugh 'til he turned as red as his hair.

"Grandma believes everything I say," Halsey sneered. "You go run home to your ugly old aunty," he added, and then stuck out his tongue and rolled his eyes. "That's what she looks like, and you, too!"

Ooh, I wanted to smack him really hard. He was bigger than me, but softer and probably slower. Bullies were usually cowards, anyway. But then I saw Halsey's purple grin widen and here came Mrs. Fowler clumping down the stairs. Her red hair was done up in a pink scarf to match her pink shorts, and she wore a big frown on her face which was directed at me.

Now was not the time to pound Halsey. Mr. Sol was right about choosing which battles to fight so as to win a war. Even so, it was hard to walk away with Halsey's braa-haa-haa laugh stinging my ears.

To calm down, I took out my special notebook and wrote a story about the turtles and a mean old sand crab (that looked like Halsey). I was getting to the really good part where a pelican swooped down to grab up that old sand crab when I saw Yuri come stalking down the boardwalk with her paints and brushes. She had her easel set up and a big canvas was all ready and waiting.

She'd started sketching what she said were studies for her new painting. Morning and night she'd been at it, until one afternoon I asked her point blank how long it took to draw an old jellyfish. She made a sound like a snort mixed up with a laugh and told me to leave her be. "I'm busy preparing, can't you see?"

Today was the day she was going to paint. Curious, I ran to ask if I could help. She said that I could carry her paints for her. "What are you going to call this story?"

I asked. She snorted again. "Well, there's a story, right? All your pictures have stories."

"Go away, Tammy," she said, sounding as if she meant business, but I stayed put and watched Yuri set up her canvas. She paid no attention to me. I sat down in the sand to watch as she spread paint. Dark blues and purples that were almost black, washes of darkest green—and now, spiraling up to the top, she added curves of almost transparent light. Like fireworks on the Fourth of July, but better. Like sunlight caught and shot through crystal. Like fire that was blazing hot but still somehow cool and far away.

It was like nothing I'd ever seen before. I didn't have words to say, and it was Yuri who finally broke the silence. "I will call this painting *The Celestial Maiden*."

The way she said it, I knew she was getting ready to tell the story. I sat quiet and waited while she picked up her blue-handled brush and stroked on more paint.

"Long ago," said Aunt Yuri, "there lived a poor young fisherman." ("Are all the fishermen in Japan poor?" I wondered. She ignored me.) "He was a handsome young man," Yuri said, "and many young women wanted to be his sweetheart, never mind that he didn't have a nice house or any furniture in it. But the fisherman wasn't interested in any of them because he was waiting for the love of his life.

"He was, in his way, a poet," Yuri broke off to explain. Then she added, "Of course not all poets are poor, but sometimes it helps."

I knew better than to ask why. Yuri was going to tell the story her way. I kept sneaking looks at the canvas, but today it was acting like an ordinary canvas.

"The young fisherman—he has a difficult name, so we will just call him Haku—liked to get up before sunup and meditate on the beach. He did this every day before setting out to sea in his rickety old boat. And each morning he would end his meditation by hoping that today would be the day he met the woman he could love forever.

"Now, on this particular morning Haku was meditating on the still-dark beach when suddenly he heard a strange and wonderful music. He'd never heard such sounds before. Did they come from a lute or a harp? He didn't know. All he knew was that the music filled his heart with joy and sorrow at the same time so that he wasn't sure whether he should get up and dance or fall down on his knees and weep.

"As Haku sat there bewildered, all of a sudden he saw something shimmering and glittering in the very faint light of that pre-dawn sky."

"There it is!" I breathed for sure enough there was a light on the canvas. Not just painted light but a brightness that grew and grew and was more beautiful than anything I'd ever seen. Holding my breath, I watched as a young man dressed in raggedy pants and an old shirt came walking across the sand.

"What could it be?" Yuri wondered. "Carefully, a little scared but terribly curious, Haku approached the shimmering object. And what do you think of this—there on a branch of a tall pine tree hung the most glorious, gorgeous and gladsome garment he had ever seen."

It was made of gold and silver and jewels and... I don't know what, but it really was something else. I didn't think there were such colors in Yuri's palette, but there she was dabbing them on with her blue-handled brush.

"Haku came closer and saw that the garment was woven of gold and silver and jewels and silks that were colored like the rainbow. Beautiful as morning and as tranquil as night. Hot like the sun and cool as the moon.

Haku lifted the robe from the tree and tenderly ran his rough fingers over the glittering fabric. He saw that sewn amongst the jewels were soft, silvery feathers. He was stroking them when a voice called softly to him.

"'Oh, please,' called that voice, 'please, young man...'"

I jumped, because the voice, that sweet, plaintive voice, had come from the canvas. Yuri's blue-handled brush had painted a beautiful woman. She was dripping wet as if she'd just been swimming, and her only covering was the thick black hair that swirled around her from head to foot.

"Please, kind young man," she was saying. "I have had a morning swim in this beautiful ocean, but now I must return to my home in the sky."

"Who are you?" Haku and I asked at the same time.

"I live in the sky. We sky people are called Celestial Maidens. I must go home..."

Don't ask me why or how, but it seemed perfectly natural that I was watching this poet fisherman telling the Celestial lady he was in love with her. "Now I know why I couldn't love any of the village girls," he said. He got down on his knees. "Stay with me ... be my wife."

The lady began to cry. "I can't," she wailed. "I have to go back home. You don't understand. Even if I wanted to stay, I can't. Going back is hard..."

I gulped down the knot in my throat. The old stories about Yuri's teacher had to be true. *She could call on the ancient spirits of earth, air and water,* that old newspaper clipping had said. Fisherman Urashima had been *water,* Little Kyu must have been *earth,* and now here was *air*—the lady from the sky— wringing her hands and pleading for her robe while poor Haku begged with her to stay on earth and be Mrs. Haku.

"But I love you," wailed Haku. "If I give you back your robe you will fly back into the sky."

He was overdoing it, but you had to feel sorry for Haku. He was sincere. The maiden knew that, I guess, because she cried so hard that her beautiful black hair bounced and swirled around her, and clouds began to fill the sky as if they were feeling sorry for her. Finally Haku couldn't stand it.

"Stop!" he cried. "Even though you will break my heart by leaving me, I love you too deeply to see you suffer." And he gave her back her robe. "You must do as you think best."

I'd thought the maiden would fly up to the sky, but she didn't. Maybe she cared for Haku just a little. Maybe she was just grateful. Anyway, she began to dance while singing Mama's song. Haku begged her to stay with him and marry him and be his love for all the days of their lives. Maybe she even thought about it a little. But she was a creature of the sky, beautiful and free and full of light. She danced across the sand and then into the sky while he stretched out his arms to her and watched as she disappeared into the clouds...

"The sun is very bright, I'll have to shift," Aunt Yuri was saying.

It was so quiet on the beach and I could hear the slap-lap of the waves. There was only one explanation for what had happened, what I'd seen and heard. Critics had called Yuri's work 'magical,' but I'd bet they hadn't seen everything. "It's magic, isn't it?" I breathed. "The blue-handled brush is magic. It calls the ancient spirits to help you paint..."

She pretended she hadn't heard me. "There is a place in Japan—*Miho-no-Matsubara*—where the Celestial Maiden is supposed to have danced. It's a famous story, one I have been wanting to paint for a long time. Inspiration did not come to me until I saw Sol-san's photograph." Yuri nodded at her canvas. "I think that it will be the best painting I have done."

The painting stood glowing in the sun. It wasn't moving or telling a story now, but just by itself it was magical. And it had secrets deep inside.

"You can do magic," I breathed.

"What is magic?" she came back. "Everything in the world is magic if you have eyes to see and a heart to feel. Do you think this old brush has magic in it? Here—you may hold it."

Gingerly, I took the blue-handled brush. The handle felt warm from Yuri's hand, but that was all. No tingle. No difference. It was just an old paintbrush. "The things I saw just now, the things in your paintings," I protested. "You *have* to do magic."

"Perhaps you are the one with the magic," she said, and flashed me one of her rare smiles. I stared at her. "You are a writer, *ne?* You breathe life into words, and they come alive for you and for others. When you write a story and make it seem real, Tammy-*chan*, that is the real magic."

Nana Honey had called me Tammy-chan, too. It was strange to hear Yuri calling me that. Strange, but kind of nice.

Chapter 13

EVEN KEN WAS IMPRESSED with Yuri's painting. Mr. Sol was blown away by it. "It's incandescent," he told her. "And you say you envisioned this when you looked at my photograph? I'm honored. And humbled."

He kissed Yuri's hand, and she actually blushed.

Mr. Sol insisted on taking us all out to celebrate that evening, so we all went to a restaurant. Mr. Sol ordered champagne for Yuri and him and sparkling cider for Ken and me. After one glass of champagne, Yuri got all red in the face and sang a funny Japanese song that made Ken laugh so hard he made me laugh, too. We giggled through the whole meal and even later when we stopped for ice cream cones on the way home.

That was a good evening. Days that followed were good, too, mainly because Dad didn't sound strained when he called, and was almost encouraging about Mama's condition. Ken had quit his efforts to be mean to Yuri, but that didn't stop either of us from being curious about her—for different reasons. Ken was still convinced that she was hiding other letters from Nana Honey in her scrapbook. Me—well, if you'd sat on the beach and watched her paintings come to life, would you be able to forget it? I was practically on fire needing to know more about Yuri and that blue brush.

So while she was out painting on the beach, we would sneak into her studio and head for the desk where she kept her scrapbook. No letters there, but plenty of newspaper clippings. Some of them were in other languages, which we couldn't figure out, but many were from England and Australia and Ireland. All of them said about the same thing about Yuri's paintings, that she seemed to have magic in her brush and paints.

I had news for them. She *did* have magic.

I kept hunting through those news clippings and finally I found a woman who'd gone to one of Yuri's painting demonstrations. *While I watched, I was spellbound,* the woman wrote. *Ms. Hamada's painting seemed to flow with life. As her blue brush darted over the canvas, I swear that I could almost see people move and birds fly.*

Bingo!

The next time Mr. Sol drove us to the library, I got on the computer and did some research. I'd written down the Japanese word that had been in that first *London Times* news clipping—*Onmyodo*—which was what Aunt Yuri's teacher was supposed to have studied. I typed in *Onmyodo* and got four pages. I skimmed them real quick and got the general idea that this *Onmyodo* stuff was a mixture of natural science and 'magical elements.' I didn't get much farther because Mr. Sol was in a hurry to leave, but that was enough for me.

I'd tried to tell Ken about Yuri's blue brush before, but he just said it was my imagination. Now that I knew about this *Onmyodo* thing, I talked him into watching our aunt putting the finishing touches on her Celestial Maiden painting. We watched for half an hour but nothing happened. Not one thing—zip—nada. Ken looked at me, made "woo-woo" sounds and circled a finger near his forehead.

It was frustrating, but there was nothing I could do except keep watching Yuri work. Meanwhile, things at turtle nest #8 were heating up. Five days before the projected 'hatch day,' Mr. Sol and other volunteers dug a trench from the nest to the sea so that the hatchlings had a runway to the ocean. They asked beachfront property owners to dim their houselights so the turtles wouldn't get turned around and head toward those lights instead of toward the sea. They then got beach chairs and sat around hoping to see the nest 'boil.'

Some nights Yuri let us join Mr. Sol, and we watched, too. We would sit quietly near the nest hoping to see a hatchling poke its little head out of the sand and get ready to head for the sea. But so far not much had happened.

Rat Weasel Halsey was still around—I could tell by the bubble-gum wrappers that I found, like bird droppings, on the beach, but we were too busy to worry about a creep like Halsey.

Then, a few days short of August, Dad didn't call. Not at seven, when he was supposed to, not at eight, not even at nine. "Something's happened to him," Ken kept saying, as we hung around the phone. "Something's got to have happened. Aunt Yuri, can't we call the police or something?"

"It could be bad traffic. Traffic is very awful in Raleigh," our aunt said, but she was worried, too, I could tell. "Let us wait a short time longer."

When the phone rang at ten thirty, I was nearest to it. "Hey, Tammy," was all Dad said, but right away I knew that something was different.

"Is Mama all right?" I gabbled.

"Let me talk to your aunt," Dad said.

Ken grabbed the phone away from me. "What's happened, Dad?"

I shoved Ken out of the way, pushing my ear against the phone as Dad's tired breath sighed through to me. "Let me talk to Miss Yuri," he repeated.

Wordless, I handed the phone to our aunt who looked a question at us and then sat down to talk. Mostly, she answered in yeses and nos, but then she said, "You don't have to worry about us, James. We are fine here. But now, you need to speak to your children."

Both of us, now, our ears pressed close to the phone receiver, listened to Dad, who said he was late in calling because he'd been at Tall Oaks all this time. "The nurses and their assistants do their best, but they're so short handed that they can't do all that's needed. I've been spending all my time away from work there, and I was there tonight."

I felt terrible. While we'd been having a good time, Dad had worn himself down taking care of Mama. My stomach rolled itself into a knot as Ken said, "We're coming home, Dad."

"No, son. Look," Dad added, "you'll be home in a couple of weeks. School's starting, remember? Might as well have fun while you can. I just wanted you to know what's going on and why I may be late in calling you sometimes. I didn't want you to worry."

"She's not going to get better, is she?" Under his tan, Ken had turned pale, and his voice was cracking wicked bad.

"We have to be prepared for the worst, son," Dad said. Before he could go on, Ken shoved the phone at me and ran out onto the deck. Yuri muttered something, grabbed up a flashlight, and went after him.

"Tammy? Ken?" Dad was saying. "I know it's hard to face—it's hard for me, too, but we have to accept God's will." Dad's voice was breaking up. I knew he was crying at the other end of the phone, just like I was crying on this side. Then he said, "When you come home, we'll go see her together, all right?"

It wasn't all right, though. We all knew that. Nothing would ever be all right again. I mumbled my goodbyes and hung up the phone. I just stood there feeling sick and lost and so scared that I couldn't even cry. I felt like I should do something, say prayers for Mama, maybe, but I couldn't think of any words except Mama's name.

After a while, Yuri came back inside looking grim. "Ken is with Sol-san on the beach," she said. Then she added, "Try not to worry about what your father said."

I knew Yuri meant well, but right then I didn't want to talk about Mama or anything else. So I ducked past her and went out onto the porch and then down the steps to the boardwalk. Tide was coming in under a full moon, and the sand was wet under my feet as I stepped down onto the dark beach.

I hardly felt the water against my ankles as I began to walk, then run along the packed-hard shoreline.

Behind me I heard Yuri calling for me to come back, but I didn't stop. I just kept on running until I was out of breath and there was a stitch in my side. Even then I kept going.

Mama was drifting away from us. Her body might still be here, but what used to be our mother was slipping away with each and every minute. She would never walk the beach, looking for shells. She would never walk into my classroom at school again or listen to me read her a story. She'd never cheer for Ken at his soccer games or laugh at Dad's jokes or ruffle our hair as she passed. I would never feel her arms around me or the soft, warm touch of her cheek on mine.

The moon was shining bright on the water. It was like a golden pathway down to the Sea King's Palace. And the sea was calling, too. I could hear the sea voices chanting: *Down deep, deep, down, down deep. Come down deep with us, for the going is so easy...*

Suddenly, the sand under my feet gave way, and I yelled as I fell forward on my hands and knees. I must have slid into one of the tide-pool hollows made by the sea, I thought as, wringing wet, I started to get back to my feet.

WHACK!

Smacked in the face by the wave, I lost my balance and fell backward. Before I could even move, another wave smashed down on me. I tried to yell, but my mouth was full of grit and water. I tried getting up but was dragged forward instead...

SWHACK!

This wave broke right over me, smashed down on me like a ton of wet cement. Flat on my back like a helpless turtle, I scrabbled to get up, and couldn't. And here came another wave, roaring and shouting with the sea-voices that seemed to be calling my name.

"Tammy, tammy, TAMMY!" Over the sea-noises I heard Ken's voice. He and Mr. Sol were coming to save me—

SMASH!

My wet clothes and shoes were dragging me down, dragging me back into the sea. The undertow scraped my arms and legs as it yanked me down deep. Then all of a sudden something grabbed onto me and started pulling me back toward shore. A wave whacked at us, but whoever had me didn't go down, didn't fall. "Hold on," Aunt Yuri's voice shouted. "Don't fight or struggle. I have you."

Sputtering, coughing, gagging, I was dragged back, pulled forward, dragged back again—and then Ken was shouting something, and big, strong hands had grabbed me by the middle, and I dropped onto wet sand. Mr. Sol was saying. "Roll on your stomach, Tammy. Roll over."

There was pressure on my back and a terrible pain in my stomach and chest. I cried as I threw up salt and sand and my dinner. "It's all right, it's all right," Mr. Sol rumbled. "Has to come out, all of it."

Ken, sounding far away and scared silly asked, "Is she okay?"

I heaved again. "She nearly drowned," Aunt Yuri replied. "What were you thinking? Walking into the sea. *Baka*—you fool, don't you know how dangerous that is? Have I not warned you never to go into the water when you were alone?"

She sounded angrier than I'd ever heard her. "Leave her alone," Ken protested, but Yuri wasn't about to stop.

"Ha! I leave her alone—she drown." Her usually faultless English was all jumbled. She grabbed my shoulders, half lifting me out of the sand, and shook me. "You worry everyone! What would your papa do if you came to harm?"

Ken grabbed hold of Yuri and tugged at her. "You let go of her!" he snarled. "You just let go, you hear?"

My teeth were chattering, and I was crying so hard that snot and tears made it hard to breathe let alone see. "That's enough," Mr. Sol was saying. "Stop that. Miss Yuri, you're not acting rationally."

"You're just mean!" Ken shouted. "You like to see people cry—like you made Nana Honey cry."

Aunt Yuri let go of me so suddenly that I fell backward on the ground. As Mr. Sol picked me up, I could hear Yuri and Ken shouting at each other. Aunt Yuri was yelling that she'd had enough of Ken's bratty behavior, and Ken was shouting right back.

"Miss Yuri, you've got to calm down." Mr. Sol's voice was stern, now. "Ken, keep that mouth of yours shut. Shut, do you hear me? Now, we've all had a shock, here..."

Without another word Aunt Yuri turned and stalked off. Mr. Sol pulled in a breath and said, "Let's get you dry and warm, Tammy. Ken, take her other arm and we'll walk her home."

"I'm not going back there, not with *her*," Ken muttered.

"Probably just as well to let you both cool off," Mr. Sol sighed. "We'll go to my house. Come on, now, easy does it."

My ears were ringing, and I felt so sick I wanted to lie down and die, but Ken wouldn't let me. He kept walking me forward, and when I wouldn't walk he dragged me. By the time we'd gotten to Mr. Sol's, the dry heaves had stopped.

Mr. Sol gave me a big towel to wrap around me and a blanket on top of it and made me drink something hot which made me want to throw up again. "Easy, now," he was saying. "Your system took a shock. That sea nearly had you, girl." To Ken he said, "Go call your aunt and tell her where you are." Ken shook his head. "Then I'll do it. I don't want Miss Yuri to worry. She saved your sister, and don't you forget that."

"I fell into a ti-tide pool," I sniffled.

Ken sat down next to me and fussed with my blanket. "You look like one of those mummies in the horror shows," he muttered. "It's okay, Tam. I know it was an accident. Yuri didn't have to jump all over you."

I put my head on Ken's shoulder, and he tried ruffling my hair the way Dad sometimes did. It was the last straw—I busted out crying. "She's never going to find the way back," I wailed. "She's not."

Mr. Sol came back into the room while Ken was trying to hush me, handed us mugs of hot chocolate and watched us while we drank. "You didn't tell me, Ken, but I guess you got some bad news tonight."

Ken explained, "Dad wants us to stay here 'til we have to start school, but we can't. We're needed back home, sir. We have to get back." Had we asked our aunt? Mr. Sol wanted to know. "It wouldn't do any good," Ken muttered. "Didn't you hear how she yelled at Tammy tonight?"

Mr. Sol said he'd heard a lot more than he'd cared to hear tonight. "You did a lot of the yelling, too," he went on, suddenly stern. "I'd like an explanation, Ken."

"She's mean, Mr. Sol. Always was. She doesn't care about anyone but herself." Then, like those waves that had whacked down on me, everything came pouring out of my brother.

Mr. Sol just listened until Ken was done. Then he sighed, rubbing his face with his big hand, thinking. "It's a sad story," he finally said. "I can see why you'd hold a grudge against your aunt. But there has to be another side of the story, too. When I had my accident and my leg was all bent upside and sideways, I was angry with the world, and I said some things and did some things I'll always regret. Hurt those who loved me best because I hurt so much myself."

"Doesn't anything make it right, what she did," Ken muttered.

Mr. Sol got up, wincing, balancing on his bad leg. "She came here to help you, didn't she? When you needed her? And it was she who jumped into the waves back there, risking herself to pull Tammy out. In her way, your aunt cares a lot about you."

He poured us more hot chocolate and watched us drink it down. Then he insisted on driving us home. I thought Ken might fuss about going back to Yuri's, but he didn't say a word.

Chapter 14

ON THE WAY BACK TO YURI'S, Mr. Sol gave us the sad news about turtle nest #8. "It happened earlier this evening just before Tammy's—ah—accident," he said. "There was a small boil—about twenty hatchlings making it out of the nest. Unfortunately, we also discovered that a ghost crab had gotten inside the nest. We got him out, but there's no telling what damage was done."

"What happens to the other eggs?" Ken was asking but without much interest.

Mr. Sol said that in cases like these, there was a seventy-two hour wait to see if any other hatchlings made it up. "Then the permit holders come and excavate the nest and see if any other hatchlings have survived," he added. It's too bad, but that's the way it goes, sometimes."

Poor turtle nest #8! My stomach clenched up, and I felt like throwing up again when I thought of those little hatchlings trapped inside their eggs. I wished there was something I could do to help them, but right now I couldn't even seem to help myself.

We just sat quietly until Mr. Sol pulled up his van in the driveway. "Here we are," Mr. Sol said. "Think I can trust you to get into the house without my coming along?"

"Yes, sir," Ken said. "Thanks, Mr. Sol."

My legs felt like they were made of cement blocks, so the climb was slow. Inside, the house was dark, though there was a light on in the studio. The door was half open, and we could see Aunt Yuri working, but when we walked past, she said nothing to us. I said something like, "We're back, Aunt Yuri," but she never even looked up.

She was really, really mad at us. Ken muttered that he didn't care. "I'm going to bed." Then he added that I stunk and better take a shower.

The shower felt hot and good and made me sleepy. I dropped into bed like a stone and woke up, startled, with sunshine on my face. My arms and legs felt like they'd been sandblasted, but otherwise I felt fine and hungry.

Ken was eating cereal when I got to the kitchen. "Where is she?" I asked.

"Gone to Morehead City to get some paints." He nodded to the note on the kitchen table. "She won't be back for a while."

Ken got up and headed toward Yuri's studio. I asked what was he doing and he threw me a scornful look, opened the door and went in. "She's already mad at us," I protested.

Ignoring me, Ken flicked on the lights just as I caught up to him. "I want to see that letter Dad wrote to her when he sent us that package. I bet she knew how Mama was doing a long time ago. She's been keeping stuff about Mama from us..."

He'd been rifling through Yuri's desk as he spoke. Now he quit doing that and started prowling around Yuri's neat studio, lifting sketchbook covers, opening drawers, fiddling with canvas. "Ken, come on," I pleaded. Yuri'll be furious if she knew we'd been messing with her stuff. "You don't touch an artist's things," I told him.

"You sound just like her," Ken scoffed. He flipped open the box where Yuri kept her brushes and pulled out the blue-handled brush. "What's she do with this thing? It looks like it's gone through the dishwasher."

"Put it down. That's her magic brush." Ken dropped the brush. He picked up Yuri's sketchbook and started skimming through the pages. Suddenly, he laughed.

"Look at this, Tam!"

Yuri had sketched old weasel Halsey and got him nailed. There he was with his mean face and sneaky expression. "If I didn't know better," Ken laughed, "old Rat Weasel could walk right out of the page."

"Hey in there..." Mr. Sol was calling at the door.

He said he was heading for Emerald Mall and thought we might like to ride along. Ken went, but I finished breakfast and then wandered out onto the porch. The sky was gray with clouds today, and there was a sharp wind blowing. I didn't want to walk the beach after what happened last night, and I wasn't about to pass the ruins of poor turtle nest #8. Most of all, I didn't want to be the only one there when Yuri came home from Morehead City. So I took my notebook and pencil and went down to our beach and sat next to the boardwalk. I tried to write about Haku and the Celestial Maiden, but as I put down words I kept thinking of Mama in billowing robes as bright as a rainbow.

Mama slowly climbing up to heaven while the rest of us called her name and held our arms out to her begging her to come home to us. Mama blowing us a kiss and telling us she loved us. 'I'm going away, now,' she's saying, and her voice is far away. 'I wanted to come back to you, but the way back is too hard. You understand, Tammy? It just is too hard to come back."

I felt so lonely that I cried. It was like all the crying I'd ever done in my life had been just baby stuff. The tears I shed for Mama now were from the bottom of my heart, the part of the heart that stays quiet and calm as long as there is someone to listen to you and tell you things will get better. There was nobody to do that now. I was just like those abandoned turtle eggs that would never, ever hatch.

I closed my eyes to try and stop the tears. I guess I must have fallen asleep because next thing I knew there were pounding footsteps on the boardwalk and Ken was shaking me, hard.

"Wake up, Tammy," he was saying, and the gaspy way he was talking sounded like he wanted to yell but didn't have the strength. "Wake up. Something's happened! No, not Mama," he added, hastily, "but real bad. Come on."

He raced away from me up the boardwalk. Groggy from sleep and tears, I followed him through the porch and house to Yuri's studio.

"No," I whispered. "Oh, no!"

The studio was a mess. The desk near the open window had been knocked over. Yuri's sketchbook had been thrown on the ground with all the sketches torn up and brushes scattered, and the Celestial Maiden had a huge streak of yellow paint right down the middle.

For one awful second I thought that Ken had done this. He must've read my mind because he got all red in the face.

"It wasn't me. I couldn't do something like this." Muttering, he started to pick up the sketchpad and the scattered brushes. "Somebody climbed through the window. I found things like this when we got back from the mall. Help me clean this up, Tam!"

There was a gasping sound, and there was Yuri just standing and staring, her face stark white, and her mouth half open. She made a rasping noise in her throat as though she couldn't catch her breath.

I thought she was going to have a heart attack or something. Ken did, too, because he started to walk toward her, but she made a push-away motion with her hands and said, "Don't touch me. Don't come near..."

She broke off into Japanese and said things which I was glad not to understand. "We didn't do this," Ken looked ready to cry.

Without a word she strode into the room and stared at the Celestial Maiden. A moaning sound came from her. "We didn't," I whispered. "It wasn't us. We came back and found everything the way it is."

"Go away, both of you," Yuri said through clenched teeth. "*Go!*" She shouted, and we got out as fast as we knew how.

We pounded down the boardwalk and down to the beach where we stopped and looked at each other. "Omygosh, Ken," I wailed, "Who could do something like that?"

"Maybe somebody trying to steal things, maybe some druggie looking for cash." Tears were rimming Ken's eyes, and he looked about as scared as I felt. Then he said, "I don't know, but Tam—you know what? I don't even blame her if she thinks I did it. The stuff I did in the beginning and that stuff I said last night..."

It was true. Disconsolately, we started scuffing our way down the beach toward the only friend we had left. We found Mr. Sol on his porch sipping coffee and listening to the radio.

"Did you hear?" he called as we climbed his stairs. "There's a front coming through. We're in for some turbulent weather, my hearties."

Then he saw our faces and broke off. "Now what?" Both of us started talking at once, and he held up a hand. "Hold it. No bad news 'til I finish my coffee."

Miserable and heartsick, I sat down on the floor and hugged my knees to my chest. Ken propped himself against the porch door, forcing his mouth not to quiver. "Here," said Mr. Sol, pouring some more coffee into his cup and handing it to Ken. "Steady your nerves, son. Nothing can be that bad."

But when we told him, his face got longer and longer, and he frowned 'til his eyes nearly disappeared. "Has your aunt called the police?" he asked.

"I ... she probably thinks I did it," Ken groaned. Mr. Sol stared at him. "I did—stuff—when we first got here. But it wasn't me this time. I'd never do that to the Celestial Maiden."

"Any idea who might be responsible?"

On the point of shaking my head, I stopped. I'd heard the scree-scraw of Mrs. Fowler's porch swing.

Ken followed my eyes. "He's a coward and a sneak. He just wouldn't dare," he muttered.

We both stared at Halsey, who was rocking back and forth as if he didn't have a care in the world. When he saw us looking, he waved at us and popped a purple bubble.

But what I was looking at wasn't purple—it was yellow. I was staring at the smear of yellow paint on Halsey's hand. It was the same color paint that we'd seen smeared across the Celestial Maiden.

Chapter 15

WHEN SOMETHING REALLY AWFUL happens, your throat can dry up on you. It took a whole half-minute before I could get out the words, and by then Halsey had slunk back into his house.

Ken was furious with me. "He saw you looking at his hands," he stormed. "He'll get it off and we'll never prove he trashed Yuri's studio. Tammy, sometimes you are so dumb..."

"Stop that this minute!" Mr. Sol shouted, really angry. "You two stay here, understand? I'm going to go over to pay a visit to Master Halsey Fowler."

He headed down the stairs, with me and Ken right behind him. "Didn't I tell you to stay put?" Mr. Sol began, but then sighed and ordered us both to stick our hands into our pockets and keep them there. "I don't want you hauling off and clobbering that boy, Ken, hear me? It won't do any good."

Grimly, we marched up the steps of the Fowler house and rang the back doorbell. After a few minutes, Mrs. Fowler came to the door. "Why, Mr. Knitsbridge," she exclaimed, and then scowled to see the two of us. "What on earth..."

Mr. Sol said he wanted a word with Halsey. After another dark look our way, she called him. My hands, obediently jammed into my jeans' pockets, itched something awful as the rat weasel came smiling into the kitchen. "You wanted me, Grandma?" he asked.

Neither butter nor sugar, not even sweet potato pie could melt in Halsey's mouth. He was Mr. Innocence, with his big, wide eyes and his big, fat grin. Ken made a strangled noise in his throat.

"Halsey," Mr. Sol said, "let me see your hands."

"Mr. Knitsbridge, I swear that you have lost your mind!"

While his grandma protested, old Halsey stuck his hands behind his back. Not quickly enough! "There!" I cried, "He's got yellow paint all over his hands! It's the same paint that he used on the Celestial Maiden."

"What is going on, here?" Mrs. Fowler shrilled. "Mr. Knitsbridge, I must ask you to leave immediately!"

Ignoring her, Mr. Sol kept his eyes steady on Halsey. "Where did the paint come from, son?"

Rat Weasel started to say something, then changed his mind. "It's on account of the model airplane, sir," he squeaked. "The one I'm painting. Would you like to see it?"

We all would. But as we started to follow Halsey out of the kitchen, Mrs. Fowler barred the way. "You are going nowhere in my house!" She stabbed a finger toward Ken. "You'd better get out right this minute before I call the police."

"We may call the police anyway," Mr. Sol said. "We have reason to believe that Halsey vandalized property belonging to Miss Yuri Hamada."

Mrs. Fowler's eyes appeared to be popping out of her head. "Vandalized," she gasped. "The idea that my Halsey could do such a thing! Why, he's been home with me all morning."

She was lying. I felt it. And here was the rat weasel with another lie—a dinky paper airplane slick with new yellow paint. "So that's what you've been working on," Mr. Sol said. Halsey nodded. "Strange that the paint on your hands is all dried while the plane is wet," Mr. Sol commented.

"That's because he just painted it!" Ken cried. "He trashed Yuri's studio!"

Halsey closed his eyes and shook his head. "Grandma, the boy is sick," he said, sadly. "Guess I have to forgive him—he doesn't know any better."

Ken shouted that he'd show Halsey how sick he was. Mrs. Fowler squealed for us to get out of her house this *minute* or else. Mr. Sol clamped one hand on Ken's shoulder, the other on mine, and steered us out the door.

Ken protested all the way. "He did it, for sure. I bet he sneaked in to Yuri's studio and saw that sketch she did of him. That made Rat Weasel mad enough to do what he done..."

Mr. Sol said, "Son, you just hold your noise and listen up."

Then he said that though he believed every word we said, there was no way we were going to get Halsey for this. "His grandmother stands by him. Says her little boy was with her all morning. That's that. For now."

Everything got real quiet. All we could hear was the whine of the wind as it whipped over the sand and through the pines along the beach. The sky had turned an iron gray, with clouds boiling up into dark thunderheads. It was setting itself up to storm all right, and soon.

"So Halsey gets away with everything, and we get blamed," I groaned.

"For now. I'm a believer in Retribution." Mr. Sol said. "It may take some time, but Halsey will get what he deserves. Meanwhile, the two of you go home."

"We can't. Yuri is..."

"I'm thinking about Miss Yuri," Mr. Sol said, sternly. "It's a terrible thing that was done to her. Her heart and soul went into her work. You go help her clean up. Help any way she lets you. Tell her what you saw on Halsey's hand. Now, go home."

But Mr. Sol hadn't seen Yuri's face when she told us to get lost. I asked if we could stay with him, but he said, no, we were needed at Yuri's.

"Make sure that you have candles and secure all the windows. We're going to have some serious weather in a little bit."

Feeling lower than any snake's belly, we made our way back onto the beach. The wind had kicked up and there were anvil-based thunderheads sweeping down from the west. The ocean looked mean.

Ken had to shout to make himself heard above the wind. "I'm not going back to the house," he told me.

"Then what are we going to do?" I started to ask, but the wind got most of my words. "We can't stay out here..."

"I'm going to Rat Weasel's," Ken said, tight lipped. "I'm going to shake it out of him." He turned to look at me over his shoulder. "You don't have to come."

Try and stop me—but when we tried to go back the way we had come, the wind was against us. Sheets of sand stung our legs and arms, and we could hardly move.

I yelled over the wind telling Ken that this was crazy, but he ignored me. Then I wailed as a huge gust of wind came spilling down at us and knocked me down, flat.

Ken hauled me to my feet just as the rain started. A skinny streak of lightning stabbed down, turning the ocean to stark white. A few seconds later, thunder boomed. Even Ken winced.

Lightning came again, this time so near and so bright the inky sky turned pink. I screamed out loud, and Ken put his arm around me, pulling me tight against him. "Okay," he conceded, "okay, we'll go to Yuri's."

It was easier walking toward Yuri's because the wind was pushing us, but the sand pelted our bare legs and the wind was a wild thing. Ken kept his arm tight around me as, heads down, we kept running. All the time the lightning was so close it seemed to be right on top of us, stabbing its crackly fingers down as if to get us.

It took several minutes, during which I screamed myself silly, before I finally spotted the bright blue door of the house. But before we could reach it hail came rattling down on top of us, big chunks of hail that made us both yelp with the sting of it.

"Run!" Ken yelled. I slipped and fell. As I fumbled around in the sand and water, I felt something hard under my hand. Without really meaning to, I grabbed it and felt stiff bristles scraping my palm.

Blinking rain and salt out of my eyes, I looked down and saw Yuri's blue-handled brush. Or saw it for one moment, before a wave wrenched it out of my hand.

Chapter 16

WHERE WAS IT? WHERE HAD IT GONE? I started searching in the wave-drenched sand. All my scrabbling fingers could find were broken shells. Ken grabbed hold of me. "Are you nuts?" he yelled into my ear while he began hauling me upright.

I shouted, no, and plopped down on hands and knees again. "I have to find it—Yuri's magic is in the brush," I half shouted, half sobbed. Rat Weasel must have thrown it onto the beach.

He'd already ruined her painting. I couldn't let him take away her magic, too! "I won't let him!" I screamed. Ken must have heard how desperate I was, because he let go of me and got down on his knees beside me.

"What are we looking for?" he shouted over the wind.

"Brush..."

Before I could get another word out, a wave whacked me in the face. All the terrors of last night came back, and I so wanted to get out of there. But, spitting out saltwater and sand, eyes stinging, I remembered how Yuri had picked up her blue-handled brush, how her hand had flown over the canvas, how she had told the story of lonely Little Kyu who had cried in the night because he wanted so much to paint. Yuri had been the one who cried...

I clamped my teeth down hard over my fear and knew that I was going to find that brush for her. I was. Nothing was going to stop me.

Then, suddenly I felt bristles against my fingers and I grabbed hold and held on tight even when another wave smacked into me. "Tam, come on," I heard Ken gasp.

He pulled me to my feet and we staggered toward the house. It wasn't until we pulled the blue door open and got inside that I looked down at the brush in my hand. And shrieked. Yuri's magic brush was broken.

A part of the handle was missing. Rat Weasel Halsey must have snapped it in two before throwing it away. I started to run back outside, but Ken grabbed me and pulled me back. "No way are you going out there," he told me. Then, he added, "Look at this place!"

The wind had roared through the open windows, caught the dishes and cups on the kitchen table and smashed them on the floor. The morning newspaper had been scattered all over the place.

There was no sign of Yuri.

"Help me get these windows shut!" Ken was slamming and banging around the kitchen, scrunching glass underfoot.

We shut and locked the windows in the big family room, and then ran down the hall to the bedrooms. We'd both left our windows open, so rain was blowing through, soaking the floor and our beds.

What about Yuri's room? Her bedroom door was closed tight. Ken hesitated, then knocked loudly. No answer. Cautiously, he opened the door to a blast of wind from the open window. The room was empty.

She wasn't in the studio, either. Yuri had shut the studio window and picked up her scattered sketchbooks, but the Celestial Maiden was still scarred. As I stared at it, I thought I saw a flutter of movement behind the horrible yellow paint as if something was trying to escape. I hated Halsey Fowler worse than snakes. Retribution, whatever that was, was too good for him.

Still no sign of Yuri. "Where's she gone to?" Ken was muttering. I said that maybe she'd gone for a walk to calm down. "Then she's caught in the storm..." Ken was chewing the inside of his lip again. "She's not from around here, she doesn't know what a storm can be like. I should go look for her."

Just then there was a blaze of light that filled the whole studio with firecracker brightness and at the same time there came an awful explosion of noise, like a house had fallen right on top of us. Then there was another sound, a ripping, tearing noise, and something smashed against the outside wall. The studio window shattered, and the lights went out.

I tried screaming, but all that came out was a squeak. Ken grabbed me and led me back out of the room into the hall where we huddled as more lightning and thunder exploded above us. "It's okay, it's okay," Ken kept saying, but his voice was cracking something awful. "Storm's passing. It's going away..."

BANG-THUD!

We both yelled aloud at the awful sound, and then, like something out of a horror show, there was Yuri running down the hall toward us. Her hair was loose and blowing in gray witch-coils all over her face. Her soaking wet dark clothes were plastered to her body. Even in the dark hall I could see the wild look in her eyes.

Had she lost it totally? Maybe so. When she saw us, she yelled something and grabbed us up and mashed us to her stammering, "You're here, oh, kind heaven, you are safe!"

And then she started sobbing, deep, wracking sobs that shook her whole body. Her sobs scared me so that I started crying. I think Ken was crying, too. All three of us stood there hanging onto each other while the thunder roared and the wind howled and screamed. Then there was another bang, and another splintering, smashing sound.

Ken pried himself loose from Yuri's grasp and said, hoarsely, that he'd go see what was going on. She held him back. "We will stay right here in the hall," she said. "Away from windows is safest right now. Later, when the storm passes, we will clean up the mess."

She sounded more like herself, and I was happy to let her have her way. For a while we were quiet listening to the storm. Then Ken asked, "Where were you?"

"I went searching for you." Yuri loosened her hold on me and stepped back to look us over. "I telephoned Sol-san, but there was no answer, so I knew you were not there. I was afraid you had decided to run away. It is what I would do after what happened today."

Even not touching him, I could feel Ken tense up. "I didn't do that stuff in your studio," he protested. "I'd never hurt the Celestial Maiden. It was..."

"Halsey Fowler. I know it. When I was cleaning the studio, I found this on the floor."

From her pocket Aunt Yuri pulled a soggy bubble gum wrapper. Ken shouted. "That's proof, isn't it? We've got the little rat weasel now!"

But Yuri said that she doubted that the police would act on a bubble gum wrapper, especially if Halsey's grandmother would give him an alibi. "Anyway," she added, "that does not matter now."

"Doesn't *matter*? Aunt Yuri, are you nuts? After what he did to us..."

"It was me who did bad things to us," Yuri interrupted, firmly. "But I must explain. I did not believe that you did this, Ken. I spoke and acted with a remembered anger over some thing that happened to me long ago. I hurled that anger on the innocent. *Honto ni sumimasen,*" she added in Japanese, then caught herself and changed that to, "I am very, very sorry."

"'S 'aright," Ken sounded embarrassed.

"Not all right. I forgot that thing I swore always to remember: the only one who can destroy our spirit is ourselves. It is a lesson I learned so many years ago."

"In Kyoto," I whispered.

"Yes, Tammy, in Kyoto." Yuri pulled in a deep breath that was not quite a sigh and let it slowly out. "I would like to explain about my life, but the story is so hard that I don't think I can bear to put it into words."

She sounded so sad that I wanted to say something to make her feel better. "You could tell it like one of your other stories," I suggested. "You know, like the story about Little Kyu and the Celestial Maiden and Taro the fisherman. As if it was happening to someone else."

For a second she was quiet. Then—"Very well," Aunt Yuri said. "But first, we must get some blankets or towels to wrap around us, *ne*? So we will not catch the pneumonia."

We raided the hall linen closet and pulled out all the towels and blankets we could find. When we'd wrapped them around us and were warm again, we settled back into the hall. Then Aunt Yuri began, "Once upon a time there was a family called the Hamadas who lived near Osaka, in Japan. There was the Father and the Mother and two sisters, Mitsu and Yuri. Mitsu was ten years older than Yuri. She used to sing Yuri to sleep with an old melody."

"The Going is Easy ..." I whispered.

Yuri nodded. "That one. Mitsu was Yuri's hero because she was so beautiful and clever and good. She was also the Father's favorite, even though he didn't show it. He was very strict and proud because his family had been Samurai many years ago under an old emperor. The Father loved Japan and didn't like western people. Then the Second World War came."

Aunt Yuri didn't say much about the war except that things were very bad and that they never had enough to eat. There were bombings every night, too. "After the war we were very poor. So Mitsu went to work for one of the Father's friends, who owned a store of fine art and antiques. One day, a young American officer came to the store to buy some gift."

"Was he handsome?" I couldn't help asking. Ken muttered something about girls having mush for brains.

"Oh, yes, handsome and good and kind—*but* he was not Japanese! When the Father found out that this American wanted to marry Mitsu, he was furious. He told her she must never see her officer again. But, because she was in love, she decided to run away from home and marry him."

Aunt Yuri was quiet for a long moment. Finally, she said, "When Mitsu left the house, her younger sister Yuri ran after her. She begged her sister not to leave her. When Mitsu refused, they quarreled bitterly and said many unkind things to each other. Yuri was only a child and could not understand about love. She felt that Mitsu abandoned her and she swore never to forgive her."

She was quiet for a long minute during which all we could hear was the howl of the wind.

"The Father made sure Mitsu was dead to the Hamadas. No one spoke of her again. But Yuri began to miss her dear sister. She wanted to beg her forgiveness for the things she's said, but because she never received a letter, she did not know how to contact Mitsu." She gave Ken a sharp look. "No Google back then, *ne*?

"But you had..." Ken broke off and Yuri went on.

"After some years, the father decided that Yuri should marry young and not grow up 'wild' like her older sister. He arranged a match for Yuri with the son of one of his friends, a much older man. But Yuri was only fifteen and didn't want to marry. She wanted to be an artist and spend her life painting."

"Like Little Kyu," I couldn't help exclaiming.

"Yes, Tammy-*chan*, like Little Kyu. Yuri's father wouldn't hear of his daughter being an artist, though. When she wouldn't marry the man he'd chosen for her, he sent her to his brother in Kyoto so that they could humble her spirit and break her will."

"That's where you got beat so bad..."

Yuri nodded. "They were cruel to me. You can't imagine how cruel! When my aunt saw me drawing pictures, she locked me in the coal shed outside the house. It was November, and cold, and all night I shivered and sobbed..."

Ken made a growly noise in his throat. I remembered what Mama used to say, that when things were really, really bad, it helped to have a hand to hold. I reached out and took hold of Aunt Yuri's cold hand and held it tight in both mine.

"I was beaten and half starved, and then one day, my aunt saw me sketching a portrait of Mitsu. She tore it up and threw all the pieces in the garbage. Then she tore up all my clothes and called me names that I cannot even now repeat."

"That's why ... when you saw the things Halsey had done, it reminded you of what your aunt did to you," Ken interrupted. "I'm sorry. I shouldn't have left the house. If I'd been here, that rat weasel would never have gotten inside."

"What is done is done. My story is nearly over, too. I ran away from my aunt and my uncle."

"Good! How?" Both Ken and I spoke at the same time, and Aunt Yuri explained that one of the servants—an old man who had tried to be kind to her—had told her of a famous lady artist who lived in Kyoto.

"I found out where this lady lived and went to her house and fell on my knees," she told us. "I bowed my head down to the ground and begged her to take me as a servant and teach me to paint. She must have thought I was a crazy person, but she didn't turn me away. Instead, she gave me paper and a brush and watercolor and told me to paint something so that she could see if I was indeed qualified to be her student..."

Right off the lady had realized Yuri's talent and taken her in. "Miss Kawana was an angel to me. She taught me how to paint, took me to Europe with her, and helped me always. When she died, she left me her studio, and her house and money, too."

So finally the story had been told. Aunt Yuri's story made up a part of the special story of our family. Someday soon I would have to write all these stories down in my special book. But Yuri was still talking.

"There was still my sister, Mitsu—your grandmother. You may ask why did I not try and find Mitsu? I thought that she had not forgiven me, that she had her own life and did not want to be reminded of the terrible past. Who could blame her? But then my mother died..."

Yuri explained that she had found one letter among her mother's things. Ken nudged me, and we looked at each other. That must have been the letter he'd found in her studio. "From it I learned everything. In the letter Mitsu told me of the many letters she had sent. She told me that you were born, and your names, and how much I would love my grand niece and nephew. I wanted to find my sister immediately, only, it was too late. Mitsu had passed away. Like the Celestial Maiden, she had spread her wings of light and air and had danced away to Heaven forever. I would never see my beautiful sister again."

Ken said, "That's why you came to see us."

"For a while I was too heartsick to do anything, but then I decided I would contact your father and try to mend this terrible thing between our families."

The wind sounded less angry now, and the storm would soon be over, but I had started to feel sleepy and didn't want to move, not even when Ken said he was going to see what was going on in the house. So I stayed where I was, pressed up against the warmth of Aunt Yuri. I guess my eyelids started to droop because after a while I heard our aunt starting to hum the familiar song. And even in my sleepy state I realized something ...

The other night when I dreamed that Mama was singing her special song, it hadn't really been a dream. It had been Aunt Yuri singing to me.

Chapter 17

THE WORST OF THE STORM WAS OVER in a couple of hours, but Aunt Yuri wouldn't let us out of the house until nearly sunset, which was when we started to clean up. A big pine tree had lost a branch and sent it smashing into Aunt Yuri's studio window. The wind had picked up a bird feeder and thrown it clear through the picture window. We got rid of the branch and temporarily blocked off the broken windows using duct tape and our aunt's roll of canvas. Then we went out on the deck to look around.

The wind had blown away most of the pots on the porch. We wanted to go down to the beach to see what damage the ocean had done. Aunt Yuri looked at the sky, which was slowly turning dark. She looked as if she was going to say, no way, but instead she sighed and told us to be careful not to go anywhere near the water.

"I am too tired to jump into the water after you today," she said. "If I did, we would all go down to the Sea King's palace—like Urashima Taro."

That reminded me about the blue-handled brush. With all that had been going on, I'd forgotten about it. I gave what was left of the brush to Yuri, and she took it and held it in both hands for a long time not saying a word.

"I'm sorry it's broken," I whispered. "It's your magic brush. You ... can you still do magic with it, can't you?"

She narrowed her eyes. "This brush is most special to me, but that is because it was given to me by Miss Kawana, the kind woman who took in a frightened, lost girl and gave her back her life."

"But I saw you paint. I know that your teacher studied *On-Onmyodo*. That's magic, isn't it?"

"The principles of yin-yang and the Five Elements ... it is too difficult to explain. *Onmyodo* was Miss Kawana's hobby, but she did not teach me magic. No one can do that." She touched my forehead with her long, slender forefinger. "True magic starts here, Tammy-chan, in the mind and heart. It is everywhere in the natural world, but only a few can see the greatest of all magics."

She was looking down at me with the dark eyes that were so much like Nana Honey's. "What is that?" I breathed.

"You will know when there is need," she said.

That was way deep, too hard to understand—almost. I followed Ken out onto the porch, but then our aunt called us back. "If going back home is what you really wish, I will take you. I will tell your father that I will stay with you in the house until it is time for you to go back to school."

It was nice of her. I told her so, and Ken added, "But it's okay. We can hang around here—it's not much more than a week 'til school. And we'll—you know—help you clean up Celestial Maiden."

"That is nice of you, also," Aunt Yuri said. "But I don't think too much real harm has been done and that I can clean away the yellow paint."

Aunt Yuri's offer didn't stay too long in our minds because that storm had done some serious damage. One of the steps leading up to the boardwalk had been washed clean away. The waves were big and angry and there on the beach were piles of seaweed and shells. I mean, big whelk shells and dozens of the biggest cockles I'd ever seen. I picked some up, sticking them into my pockets as we hurried toward Mr. Sol's house.

We ran as fast as we could down to Mr. Sol's. He was sitting out front and greeted us with a big smile. Then he squinted across the now dark beach. "That looks like your aunt," he said. "Are you two in trouble again?"

"No, sir!" But it sure was our aunt, and she was walking so fast as to be nearly running and waving as if she wanted to flag down a train.

All three of us began walking toward Aunt Yuri. Seeing us coming, she stopped and put her hands on her knees and waited, all out of breath.

"You're out of condition," Ken scolded as we ran up to her. "You shouldn't walk that fast. You could pass out or something."

She cut him short. "We have to get back to Raleigh right away," she said.

I felt as if I'd fallen down a thirty-storey elevator. Ken licked suddenly dry lips. "Is—Mama's not *dead*?"

"What? No, no, she's not—" Aunt Yuri took a gulp of air and spoke really fast. "Your mother woke up from her coma this evening. She opened her eyes!"

Chapter 18

"OPENING THE EYES is a reflexive movement. It doesn't necessarily mean that your mother is recovering."

Aunt Yuri warned us this way as we ran around the house pulling on dry socks and sneakers. "Do not get your hopes up," she added.

"But you said we should believe in things even when nobody else would," I reminded her. "Remember the Ginger Seller?"

Aunt Yuri stopped in her tracks, turned around and put her arms around me. She held me really tight. "You are right," she said, "and I am wrong. *Ne?* Of course there is magic in the world, if we believe."

Ken watched us impatiently. "How long will it take us to get to the hospital?"

For once we didn't mind the way Aunt Yuri drove. Let her weave in and out of traffic—let that man in the eighteen-wheeler bleep his air horn and shake a fist at us. Not one wince came from us, not one protest.

Face set tight like rock, hands gripped tight around the wheel, our aunt put the pedal to the metal. We rocked back and forth in our seat belts and Ken finally said, "Ah, Aunt Yuri? If you get caught, you're going to lose your license, probably."

"I am not caring," said our defiant aunt in her worst English yet. "It is for good cause, *ne?* I am thinking that this one time end justifies means."

We loved her.

So we wove in and out of traffic and I closed my eyes and prayed. *I believe. I believe, please, please, I believe!*

When we were on the dark highway and skimming along, Aunt Yuri told us about Dad's call. "It came about half an hour after you left," she related. "I had just finished cleaning the paint off the Celestial Maiden when James phoned. He sounded as if he had trouble breathing, so I was scared until he told me that the hospital had called him. They said only that your mother had opened her eyes. He was out of the room at the time, and he did not see it with his own eyes, but still, it happened."

Ken and I high-fived in the back seat. "I am praying to see Mitsu's daughter smile at us." Aunt Yuri's voice cracked on a sob. I felt my eyes water up, and Ken sniffed hard and wiped his nose on the back of his hand. Then he cleared his throat a couple of times and managed to ask how the Celestial Maiden was.

"After what Halsey did, can you save her?"

"I will save," said our aunt, firmly. "These people like Halsey Fowler—and my father, and my aunt in Kyoto—the world is full of them. But they can't beat us unless we let them. *Ne?* Little minds and mean actions—they cannot really touch us."

"But *still* ..."

"Your Shakespeare says, 'For I am armed so strong in honesty, that your words pass me by like the idle wind, which I regard not.' Wise man, Shakespeare. I saw his play when I was in England with Miss Kawana ..."

I didn't know about Shakespeare—our class had gone to see *Romeo and Juliet* one time, and there'd never been anything like what Aunt Yuri was saying—but Ken seemed to get what she was talking about.

"They can sure make it ugly, though," he said.

"Because they are ugly in their hearts. But no matter. There will always be Halsey Fowlers, but there is only one Yuri. Only one Tammy and Ken Jennings."

The road flew by us, and we were all quiet in the car. Ten minutes, half an hour, an hour, an hour and a half... Ken began cracking his knuckles. It drove me crazy. "How much longer?" I kept asking, and every time Aunt Yuri said, "A few miles less than when you asked me last. We have a long way to go, yet."

At last, we saw our exit sign. Ken yelled out, "Finally," and started chewing on his fingers. Aunt Yuri slowed marginally down as she negotiated the difficult twists and turns to Tall Oaks.

Then, we were in the parking lot. Now that we were here, my legs didn't want to move. I was scared. Supposing that Mama's opening her eyes didn't mean anything? *I believe, I believe*—but supposing there was nothing left to believe in, no magic left in the world? Supposing Aunt Yuri's magic brush never made a canvas dance with life ever again?

Aunt Yuri had said that Dad would meet us in Mama's room, so we took the elevator up to the third floor. Visiting hours must have been over, but we paid no attention at all and hurried past the nurse's station to the room. The door was closed. We'd been in a hurry all this time but now, suddenly, we began to walk more slowly.

"Well," Aunt Yuri said and looked at us. "Now, it is the time."

"Yeah," Ken said, his voice breaking on the word.

Aunt Yuri held out her hand to me, and I took it. "You are the man of the family. You lead the way," she told Ken. So he tapped on the door, opened it, went inside.

I was about to follow, when Aunt Yuri held me back. "The greatest magic, Tammy... it is time for you to know what it is." Impatient to follow Ken, I tried to shake off her hand. "It is in the moment when you think of the other, not of yourself. It is in the song that brings back memories of love." Her hand gripped mine harder. "It is in believing when there is nothing left to do but to believe. Do you understand?"

Not waiting for my answer, she drew us both through the door and into Mama's hospital room. Mama's eyes were closed. She looked like she'd looked before we went away, with her dark eyelashes lying like dark fans on her pale cheeks. Dad was sitting on the chair by

Mama's bed. Just sitting, his head bent forward, his hands on his lap.

"Dad?" Ken's voice cracked sharp on the word.

He didn't get up, didn't come over to us. "No change," he said, wearily. "There's been no change since I came. I shouldn't have jumped the gun and phoned you," he added, sadly. "The doctor came by just now. He says..." his voice broke. "If she recognizes us, if she responds, then there's a chance, a very good chance that she'll be okay. But even then, it will take time, and I don't know how..."

"There is no 'how,'" said Yuri, firm and sure. "I will stay and help until my sister's daughter recovers fully. All will be well. You will see."

"It could have been just a reflex," Dad said, so low you could hardly make out the words. "I should have waited to see if it meant anything."

We'd hurried down here for nothing. A sob worked into my throat, but I pushed it down because Dad looked so tired. I ran to him and hugged him, and then Ken came, and Dad held him, too.

What was there to say? So we didn't say anything.

Then I heard Yuri singing, softly. I looked up, sharp, and there she stood by Mama's side. She was stroking

Mama's hand and leaning down, singing the song that her big sister had sung to her so many years ago.

"Going is easy, returning is scary—"

Pulled by that sweet-sad melody, I let go of Dad and walked over to Mama's bed and took her other hand. It was soft and warm. When I leaned up against the bed and put my face against Mama's cheek, her cheek was warm, too. "Wake up," I whispered. "Please, please, come back to us. I know it's hard. I know the road back can be scary. But I know you can make it if you try. If you believe..."

Ken was there talking to Mama, too. Above his voice and mine Yuri's husky voice sang the melody that Nana Honey had taught Mama to sing to us. When I began to hum it, too, Yuri's hand settled on my shoulder, her grip warm and firm.

Magic is everywhere, Tammy, but only a few can see the greatest magic.

But magic hadn't been enough for Fisherman Taro who had left the Sea King's palace because he wanted to be with his family. I thought of Little Kyu who wanted to draw more than anything. And Haku who loved the maiden from the sky so much that he let her leave him even when that broke his heart.

The greatest magic in the world was *love*. I closed my eyes and believed in my love for Mama. While Aunt Yuri sang and Ken talked, I just kept believing in that.

Then, after a time, Dad said my name, and my heart went down to the floor because I knew he meant that it was no use and that we had to quit. But I wouldn't stop, not while Aunt Yuri kept singing. Then—"Tammy," Dad said again, and this time there was a change in his voice.

Not wanting to, I opened my eyes and saw that Mama's eyelashes were fluttering. Slowly, they opened.

"Lily," Dad said, hoarsely, "Lily, are you awake? Do you know who we are?"

Mama's eyes were open, but they didn't focus, they just stared into the shadows of the room. Maybe it was just a reflex after all. I wanted to burst into tears but instead I began to sing our song again.

And I thought—*Mama, if the way home is too hard and you can't find your way back, don't worry about us. You're our Mama and I will love you forever.*

Mama blinked.

Aunt Yuri went quiet, but I kept on singing. Now the words Nana Honey had taught us were coming back to me. And while I sang them the magic was so strong that I could almost see the Ginger Seller shouting with joy to find his gold mine, and Fisherman Taro running to meet his dear family, and Little Kyu painting with Tama purring nearby, and the beautiful Celestial Maiden bending down to take Haku's hand and lift him up with her into the blue sky.

I love you, Mama ... always and always, never mind what happens...

And here was our mother looking straight at me. I thought I saw something move in her eyes ... some light, some flicker of understanding. I hoped—prayed—*knew*—that she saw me. But before I could even put a name to it, the light was gone.

Chapter 19

WE DIDN'T WANT TO LEAVE Mama, not for a second. We stayed while doctors came in and examined her and talked quietly to Dad, saying that there was a possibility that opening her eyes was a hopeful sign and that the best thing we could do for now was to let her rest.

"You need your rest, too," Dad told us. "Go home and get some sleep. Miss Yuri will go with you. I'll stay here for a bit."

Ken says that I was out like a light before we even got to Aunt Yuri's car. I guess that was true because the next thing I remember is bright sunshine and Yuri's voice talking on the phone. I opened my eyes and saw that I was in my own bedroom, not at the beach but in my own bed, and sunlight was dancing through the curtains that Mama had sewed for me.

Mama. I jumped out of bed and ran out into the kitchen where Aunt Yuri was just hanging up the phone. "Did anything happen?" I cried.

Her smile made her look like Nana Honey again. "That was your papa. He came home late last night and slept a few hours. He has gone back to sit with your mother. There has been no change, not yet. You must be patient."

Ken came yawning into the kitchen then, and Yuri had to repeat everything she had said to me. "There is nothing I can do here this morning," she went on. "So, I was thinking..." she paused, searching our faces. "I was thinking that I would drive back to Emerald Isle this morning. The house is not secure because of the broken windows. I am afraid of leaving my artwork there for too long."

She didn't mention Rat Weasel Halsey, but I knew she was thinking about him. "I must also speak with the landlord about the damage from the storm," she went on. "I can leave now, and be back by tonight."

And the turtles. What had the storm done to the turtles? With everything that had happened, I'd forgotten all about turtle nest #8. Now I pictured it all messed up by the wind and the waves. I wanted so badly to go and see that nest. At the same time I couldn't stand not being with Mama. I didn't know what to do. Maybe Aunt Yuri read the indecision in my eyes, "If you wish you could ride to the beach with me. We would stay only to pack. We could be back by this evening."

I looked at Ken. He shrugged. "You're going to need help with the canvasses and stuff," he said to our aunt.

Aunt Yuri nodded gravely. "That is so. I would appreciate help. Let us phone your papa and see what he says to this plan."

When we phoned Dad, Mama was asleep. He said that she'd opened her eyes again while the doctors were examining her. "The doctors didn't exactly say so," he went on, "but they seem more hopeful. I think there's been some progress." Then he added since there was nothing we could do at Tall Oaks anyway, we should definitely go with Aunt Yuri and give her a hand.

We were pretty quiet on our way back to Emerald Isle. Traffic was heavy on I–40 East, so even Aunt Yuri had to pay attention to driving. Ken had his eyes closed even though I knew he wasn't asleep. I kept thinking about Mama and ... the turtles.

Maybe they'd already hatched—but my heart sank as we came closer to the beach. Last night, we hadn't been paying attention to anything but going to Mama, but now we could see how much damage the storm had done. Many trees had toppled, and the drainage ditches were full with rainwater that sloshed across Coastguard Road.

Yuri looked worried. "I am hoping that the rain did not get into the studio and damage my sketchbooks," she sighed. "I would hate to lose them."

"It'll be okay," Ken reassured. "Me and Tammy will get everything out. Just tell us what to do."

Packing Aunt Yuri's supplies and helping to wrap her paintings took a chunk of time. We three then worked to clean up the glass from broken windows and sweep and vacuum the floors. By the time we carried out the paint-spattered Celestial Maiden, it was getting dark.

"I could not have done this without you," our aunt told us as the three of us managed to maneuver that big canvas into the car. "Now, I have an idea. We must eat before we drive back to Raleigh, so let us ask Sol-san to have dinner with us."

All afternoon while I carried and packed and cleaned, my mind had been slipping back to turtle nest #8. Here was my chance to find out what had happened to it. "We could run down to his house and ask him," I offered.

Ken beat me down to the beach, but he slowed enough so that I could catch up to him. "Do you think any more turtles made it out?" I panted.

"I don't know, Tam, but Mr. Sol can tell you. Hey— there he is!"

Close by the water, nearly bent over double, our friend was training his camera toward the waves. His back was to us, and he didn't hear us hollering his name until we were a few feet away. When he finally turned around, he looked relieved.

"I was wondering what happened to you," he exclaimed. "Went by your aunt's house last night, but the place was locked up and dark as pitch. Where did you go?"

When we told him, he nodded thoughtfully, and said that healing often took time. "You can tell me more over dinner," he added. "Hang on and I'll go change my shirt," he said.

I stopped him as he was hurrying off. "Mr. Sol, what happened to the other eggs in nest #8?"

His sighed a little and he shook his head. "Nothing after that first boil, Tammy. There was a strong storm surge last night, and—I'm sorry."

The beach was quiet except for the boom and slosh of waves busy with their song. There was an ache in my heart. Under the sand there were many little turtles that would never hear the call of the sea.

Chapter 20

AT DINNER NOBODY SEEMED TO NOTICE that I didn't say or eat much. Aunt Yuri and Mr. Sol talked almost nonstop to each other. Ken was so hungry after working all afternoon that he was totally into his food. He gulped down his dinner and most of mine, too, while the grownups went on and on about light and shadow and cloud formations.

You would have thought that they'd talked themselves out, but after dinner Mr. Sol was still going strong. "I'd like you to see my latest work, Miss Yuri. That is, if you have time."

She hesitated, then nodded. "I promised that we would return to Raleigh tonight, but a few minutes will not matter. I would like to see," she said. Then, when Mr. Sol offered her his arm, she looked pleased and took it.

They were still talking when we got to Mr. Sol's house, so I said I was going to take a quick walk on the beach. The sea was at half tide and looked dark under the overcast sky. I slipped off my sneakers and wriggled my toes in the cool sand, waiting for Ken to come up beside me.

"I'm going to miss this place," he sighed.

I would, too. "Remember when we hated the thought of coming here?" I asked.

We started walking, scuffing sand as we went. "Mr. Sol says that we're going to keep in touch," he said after a while. "He knows I want to be a photo journalist. He says he'll help me any way he can, and ... hey, what's going on?"

Someone not far from us was making a lot of noise. Curious, we hurried down the beach. As we ran, the shouting got louder and more familiar. Now even through the darkening twilight we could recognize Mrs. Fowler in some kind of billowing green housecoat.

"You see what I'm seeing?" Ken gasped.

Mrs. Fowler had Halsey by the shoulders and was shaking him fit to rattle his teeth into his brains. This being too good to miss, we ran faster than before. Soon we could hear Mrs. Fowler shrieking at her precious grandson. "I can't believe it," she was screaming.

"The idea. The very idea that a grandson of mine could do such a terrible thing. Halsey Jameston Fowler, how could you?"

Halsey was struggling to get away from his grand-mother. "I didn't, I didn't!" he was squealing. "It was the storm, Grandma..."

"And that's why I found you kicking in the sand near the nest?" Mrs. Fowler bellowed. "Is that why I find your horrible bubble-gum wrappers littering the beach at the site of the nest #8? You are a wicked child!" Then off she went telling Halsey that this was the thanks she got for taking him away from the city for the summer and how she had nursed a serpent in her bosom.

Mrs. Fowler was louder even than the brass section of the band in our school as she commenced dragging Halsey up the steps. When he held back, she smacked him and shouted that he was a disgrace to the family and that by messing up turtle nest #8, he'd committed a federal crime. By the time she'd hauled him to the top of the stairs, old Rat Weasel Halsey was bawling his eyes out.

Ken said that it was a right pretty sight. "Those bubble gum wrappers Rat Halsey left all over the beach must've blown into nest #8. She thinks he did it on purpose!

Retribution," he added, quoting Mr. Sol. "Oh, man, is Halsey ever getting retributed!"

But I wasn't listening to Ken. I was looking at the sorry patch of sand that was all that was left of our turtle nest. The trench that the volunteers had dug was gone, and wind and waves had washed away posts and flags marking the site of nest #8. There was nothing left to mark the spot.

Back in May, Mama Turtle had dragged herself out of the sea and laid her hundred-plus eggs. We had all helped to watch and guard that nest for all this time. Now, our watch was over. Thanks to the storm and the hungry ghost crabs the little turtles would never hatch.

It was so sad. I got down on my knees beside what had been #8. Ken began, kindly, "At least some of them hatched, Tam..." but I interrupted him.

"Look!" I breathed.

I was staring at little ripples in the sand near the nest. Little ripples, and then a push and a shove. A tiny flipper popped out of the sand.

Ken knelt beside me as more of the tiny hatchling appeared. Not more than a couple of inches, it was brown with darker brown flippers. And with those flippers it was pushing itself out of the sand.

Ken whispered something under his breath. Then he yelled for me to stay put. He was going to get Mr. Sol. He raced away, but I got to work scooping sand with my hands to make a trench for the hatchling. While I worked, I kept an eye out for any crab that might dare to come along.

Meanwhile, the hatchling was busy. Push, push, went those tiny flippers, as he pushed himself away from the ruins of nest #8 and started down the trench I had made. Now I saw another tiny head break out of the sand. Another hatchling was on its way up!

My shout brought Ken running down the beach with Mr. Sol and Aunt Yuri behind him. Mr. Sol had his camera, of course, but he'd forgotten his Red Sox baseball cap and his hair was standing every which way on the top of his head. As he knelt down with us on the sand, a third little hatchling popped out of the sand. It was paler than the other two, and its tiny fins had whitish rims.

Mr. Sol started clicking away with his camera. I was still on my knees, following the tiny hatchlings on their trek down to the ocean. "That's it, go with them," Mr. Sol approved. "They have to find their way to the sea."

There was so much sand and the hatchlings were so little. The sea was far off—but did that stop them?

No, sir, it did not. Their flippers made tracks like tiny bulldozers, and they were on their way. The first little guy that had come out of the nest thought he was the boss of everyone. You could almost hear him shouting, "Follow me, y'all!" as he took off wriggling and flipping down my trench toward the sea.

Holding my breath, I followed and watched. Here came a squealing seagull—and I shooed it away. I scared off a bunch of hopeful ghost crabs, too—they'd done enough damage! The hatchlings didn't even pay attention. There they went, all of them, without any kind of hesitation. No, sir. They knew where they were going, all right!

Then the little guys slid into the surf. They had no fear at all, not even when the dark, stormy waves crested over them.

"It's their home, the ocean," Mr. Sol said. He'd come to stand beside me. "It's where they are meant to be."

I stood up and dusted off my knees. "Will they make it?" I asked.

"There are predators out there in the ocean, and snares. But I'm thinking that these hatchlings will make it to the Gulf Stream just fine. They'll find rafts of sargassum to hide in until they grow a bit. Then they'll migrate to forage in shallow coastal waters."

Ken now came up, following another hatchling, a latecomer who was moving like crazy to catch up to the others. "And then what?" he asked.

Mr. Sol said he didn't know. "I've heard that some turtles will stick to the muddy bayous and bays of the Gulf Coast. My guess, though, is that these guys are heading for the clear, beautiful waters of Macaronesia—the Azores, Madeira, the Canary Islands—where they'll grow and grow. They're listening to a song that Mother Nature put into their little turtle brains. They're heading *home!*"

"Like Fisherman Taro's little turtle," Aunt Yuri murmured. She'd come to stand behind me, her hand on my shoulder. I nodded, feeling so happy I was almost ready to cry.

"Bye, you guys!" I called, and then felt silly. But nobody laughed, not even Ken.

We'd seen four hatchlings come out of turtle nest #8. "It's exciting," Mr. Sol kept saying. Then he added, "We hadn't expected much out of this nest after the crab infestation and the storm. I'll go back to the house right now and call the other members of the committee and get them down here..."

He broke off and turned to face Aunt Yuri. "I know you have to go back now, but we must stay in touch." She nodded, her eyes bright in the dim light. "You'll phone me when you get to Raleigh so that I know you've got there safe?"

"I will phone. Until we meet again, Sol-san."

Mr. Sol and our aunt eyed each other for a long moment. Then Mr. Sol reached out awkwardly, took one of Yuri's hands and kissed it. "Until we meet again, Miss Yuri," he agreed.

Then he threw back his head and gave a joyous whoop. That happy noise was like a signal that set me and Ken free to run like we'd never run before, to make tracks down the sand as if we were loggerhead hatchlings finally on our way to the sea.

Acknowledgements

Grateful thanks to Sea Turtle Biologist Matthew H. Godfrey; to Michael Coyne, Director of Seaturtle.org; to Jenifer Odom, Educator at the Aquarium at Pine Knoll Shores, North Carolina, and the Aquarium's kind volunteers who answered my many questions about loggerhead turtles.

Loving thanks also to my aunts Juliette and Francine who, long ago, taught me how folksongs and tales bring color and life to the past.

About the Author

Maureen Crane Wartski is an award-winning novelist who was born in Ashiya, Japan, in a house by the sea. As a child, she listened to stories and folktales told by her aunts, and these folktales as well as an early introduction to classical literature have influenced many of her young adult and middle-grade novels. Her Eurasian heritage and a deep connection with the natural world add flavor to her writing. She and her husband make their home in Raleigh, North Carolina, but spend as much time as possible at their beach house on Emerald Isle—within the sounds of the sea.

Sea Turtle Conservation

North Carolina Sea Turtle Project
www.seaturtle.org/groups/ncwrc

Seaturtle.org
www.seaturtle.org

International Sea Turtle Society
www.seaturtlesociety.org

The Karen Beasley Sea Turtle Rescue and Rehabilitation Center
www.seaturtlehospital.org

Sea Turtle Fun Facts

Where do sea turtles live?
Sea turtles can be found in waters of every state on the Eastern Seaboard, from Maine to Texas. Nesting occurs only in southern states, including southern VA, NC, SC, GA, FL, AL, MS, LA and TX.

How many eggs are usually laid in a sea turtle nest?
For loggerhead turtles, the average number of eggs laid per clutch (nest) is 120.

How many out of a "typical" nest actually hatch?
Under optimal conditions, approximately 90% of all eggs produce hatchlings. However, out of 1,000 eggs, only one hatchling will reach maturity on average.

What are dangers to sea turtles?
Habitat loss (both terrestrial for nesting and marine, where they spend almost all their time), pollution, incidental capture in fisheries, disease.

What can kids do to help sea turtles?

Reduce your impact on the environment, reduce, reuse, recycle, volunteer with or make a donation to a nonprofit group working with turtles.

Why are sea turtles important?

Sea turtles are important because they serve as important components of the marine ecosystem, including: regulation of seagrass beds, transfer of energy and nutrients from the ocean to the dunes, and maintenance of diversity in coral reefs.

How do sea turtles know where and how to return to their birth regions to lay their eggs?

This is one of the great mysteries of sea turtles.

Do they lay eggs every year?

Kemp's Ridley and Olive Ridley species often produce eggs in successive years, but other species usually lay eggs every second year or so.

How long do sea turtle eggs take to hatch?

The length of incubation depends on the sand temperature—in the middle of the summer when the sand is hot, it can take only 50 days; in late summer or early fall, eggs may take as long as 80 days to produce hatchlings.

How old do sea turtles usually have to be to lay eggs?

For loggerheads, it takes about 35 years for turtles to reach maturity.

How many different kinds of sea turtles are there? What are their names?

There are seven different species in the world:

Loggerhead sea turtle	Kemp's Ridley sea turtle
Green sea turtle	Olive Ridley sea turtle
Leatherback sea turtle	Flatback sea turtle
Hawksbill sea turtle	

Have any gone extinct? What kind are the most endangered and why?

There are fossil remains of many different kinds of sea turtles that no longer exist. One was called Archelon and was much bigger than any sea turtle species existing today: the biggest fossil is 16 feet from flipper to flipper. All sea turtles in the US are listed under the Endangered Species Act, meaning they are considered to be threatened with extinction. The Kemp's Ridley sea turtle is likely the rarest species, because it nests almost exclusively in a small region in the northwestern Gulf of Mexico.

What does a sea turtle biologist do?

Work towards protecting and understanding sea turtles.

What do sea turtle volunteers do?

Volunteers often help monitor and protect sea turtle nests, or they may help respond to dead or injured turtles found along the coastline, or they may work in rehabilitation centers designed to help injured or sick turtles recuperate.

What are good things to study to become a marine or sea turtle biologist?

Biology, marine ecology, physiology, policy, conservation.

How small are sea turtles as hatchlings? How large do they grow? How many years do they live on average?

Sea turtle hatchlings can fit in the palm of your hand. Most adult sea turtles weigh more than 200 lbs, although some species can weigh more than 800 lbs. The age of maturity for all species is unknown, but some can take as long as 35–40 years to reach maturity. We don't know how long they can live after that, although some tagged individuals have been observed nesting for more than 20 years.

How many miles do they swim between their birth beaches and their feeding and mating grounds?

Some individuals may cross entire ocean basins between feeding and mating.

Do sea turtles migrate annually?

As adults, male sea turtles usually migrate between their feeding grounds and nesting grounds every year, but females migrate between these areas only during years when they are going to reproduce. Before they reach adulthood, sea turtles often migrate to different developmental areas, depending on their size.

How fast do sea turtles swim?

Sea turtles can swim quickly, especially if they are trying to evade predators. During migration, they may average speeds of 3 to 4 km/hr, which allows them to traverse great distances within several weeks.

What do they eat?

The prey of sea turtles depends on the species. Green turtles tend to eat seagrass or algae, Leatherbacks eat different types of jellyfish, hawksbills tend to eat sponge and coral, and loggerheads, Kemp's Ridleys, Olive Ridleys and flatbacks are carnivorous and eat mollusks and crustaceans.

Who are their predators?

Sea turtle predators vary with the age and size of the turtles. Hatchling turtles may be eaten by land crabs, sea gulls, and many different types of fish. Once turtles reach adult size, there are fewer predators that can threaten them. Nevertheless, adult turtles may be predated upon by sharks, killer whales, and even jaguars on nesting beaches.

What's the difference between a sea turtle and regular land turtle?

Sea turtles are specifically adapted to life in the marine environment, including streamlined shells and flippers. Also, marine turtles have lost the ability to retract their heads in their shells.

How old is the sea turtle species? Were they here around the time of the dinosaurs?

The first turtle species in the fossil record showed up about 200 million years ago. Modern sea turtles appeared 120 million years ago, during the age of dinosaurs.

Information courtesy of Matthew H. Godfrey, PhD, Biologist, North Carolina Wildlife Resources Commission; North Carolina Sea Turtle Project

Sleepy Hollow Books

Sleepy Hollow Books is an independent children's book publishing company based in Durham, North Carolina. Our promise is to strengthen children's connection to nature and to foster a sense of wonder, hope and possibility. Subjects of interest include folk and wonder tales, stories about nature spirits, intuition, and other highly imaginative topics.

Sleepy Hollow Books was formed and founded by Amy C. Spaulding, who also serves as our publisher. We believe that all children are gifted, that every voice deserves to be recognized and heard, and that our planet is our greatest teacher.

To learn more about Sleepy Hollow Books, please visit our website at www.sleepyhollowbooks.com.